WATER

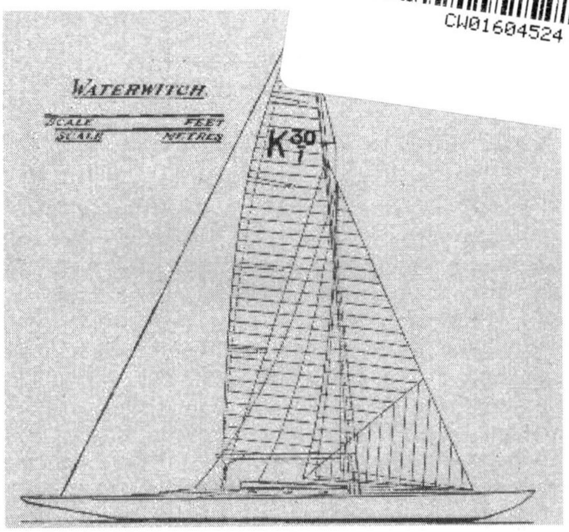

WATERWITCH was a Thirty-Square Metre built in 1937 by Uffa Fox to a design by Knud Reimers.

Fox used this experience to develop his design for Sea Swallow in 1938.

The boat is recorded in Uffa Fox's 1937 book: "Racing, Cruising and Design"

Thirty square metre yachts are featured in Fox's 1938 book: "Thoughts on Yachts and Yachting".

Length Overall	43'-6"
Length WL	28'-6"
Beam Max	7'-2"
Draught	4'-11"
Sail Area in square feet	323
Displacement in tons	2.75

Waterwitch

Chapter One

The Storm in a Metal Boat

The sixteen-ton sailing boat, Oreana, surfed over the gigantic waves. Its metal hull thudded into the swell. The steel construction prevented the boat from breaking up but it was this heavy material that within minutes of flooding would sink to the ocean floor faster than a stone thrown into a pond. Our vulnerability, the smallness of our fifty two foot boat in such a vast, turbulent and unpredictable ocean, occupied all our minds. The Atlantic in a gale is cold and very lonely even if there are four crew members on board. We had managed to haul down the mainsail and start the engine but the jib remained hoisted, its ropes loose flapping in the wind. How I wished I was back in Olhao, still sleeping on Waterwitch.

Safety, which was the Portuguese coast, lay twelve miles away and it was becoming farther away with every wave. We were being driven west towards America with only two days water on board. The Azores laying to the south west might as well have been equally as far away. We had no control over the boat as wind and waves pushed us further out to sea.

Cloud hung in a stratus layers in all directions of the compass, the rain fell diagonally towards us, hitting us on the back of the head. Waves crashed over the bow as we bobbed helplessly into the shipping lanes. Waves ten metres high raised us above the blue, green boiling water below. We seemed to rest on the foaming crest, allowing sometimes a glimpse of a container ship or tanker, but mostly the grey cloud horizon, before plunging down into the swirling cauldron. Sliding along the wave would bring the boat into a deep trough where another wave would crash over the bow as our boat dipped into the bubbling green, grey brine.

As the boat perched again on the peak of a wave, our Captain, Geoffrey, spoke, "That jib needs to come down; you'll find a harness below."

He had to shout to be heard above the roar of the wind, holding the tiller with both hands to fight the undercurrents. I stood with one leg resting on the starboard bench, trying to catch my breath. In a heartbeat, we were lifted up again on the swell and as it grew higher, we floated up like a chair on a Ferris wheel. This undulation took us forward by twenty metres in what seemed like as many seconds. There was no other description for it, we were storm-surfing. The sensation was slightly unsettling; like being in an express lift constantly going up and down.

"If you want that jib down you can take it down yourself," I replied. "I was almost swept over the side taking down the mainsail."

The jib tugged at the jib sheets, the ropes that controlled the front sail, it twirled itself around the forestays or danced in the wind like a kite, the only problem was the constant racket it made. The manic flapping became a muted clapping as the jib wrapped itself around various wires on the deck, before spinning off the wire and flapping like mad again. The noise was annoying, but it was not a danger to anything but our nerves. As the sail material got damper, the sound got worse, almost like a continuous cracking. As we dipped into a wave, the noise abated slightly but as we rose to the top of the windswept crests it became almost deafening. I could tolerate the noise if it meant me remaining relatively safely in the cockpit.

"We'll leave it," he hissed through clenched teeth. Perhaps by refusing to follow his order, I had exposed his own reluctance to move forward; after all he had not volunteered to take the jib down in my place. I had not intended to expose his cowardice; I was merely relieved that I did not have to risk my life again.

Our boat was a heavy fifty-two foot sailing cruiser; it was not built to be buffeted by waves three times it size. It was brilliantly suited to day sailing in safe seas near the coast and coping with the occasional anchorage overnight beyond the safety of harbour but it was totally unsuitable for the open sea. The sea rose and fell around us and we bobbed up and down with it, the boat dwarfed by the swirling, bubbling swell. Our engine, our rudder and sails were useless defences against the onslaught of nature.

Even as an inexperienced sailor, I had heard of boats broken in storms in the Bay of Biscay, it was a notoriously dangerous part of the Atlantic. I had never heard of storms so bad in this part of Atlantic, the Cabo da San Vincent, Faro and the Golfo de Cadiz were synonymous with sun and sandy beaches. Our storm was a perfect storm, a perfectly and absolutely petrifying storm, straight form the Bay of Biscay, all rain, high seas and spray.

There I stood, in the cockpit, soaked to the skin, every fibre of my cotton polo shirt clogged with water, the material sticking to my wet flesh. My denim shorts felt twice as heavy with the water they had absorbed. This was not what I had expected when I agreed to go sailing for the day. Sanctuary, Vilamoura, our original destination, lay shrouded in the mist to the south east of our present position. We had been forced by the wind and waves to over-shoot the harbour, the elements had thwarted our escape, but I was too scared to worry about that. I just wanted us to remain floating. I felt sure the storm would abate eventually.

We were in a frosted bowl of fierce activity; a canopy of grey surrounded us above, while below the sea bubbled, swirled and foamed, flicking cold flecks of salt water over our prow. Our ship was shaken by the constant battering. I was only nineteen but I knew real danger and recognised it now. I was cold and could feel the water drip off my brow and sodden clothes. My legs were as wet as if they had been in a shower. I felt water run down my neck. My hair was so wet that I had to flick my head to shake off the excess water so I could see and every five minutes my hair was washed forward over my eyes and I had to run my fingers through the lank strands to clear the hair from my eyes.

"Take the tiller," commanded Bill. "I'm going down below. Make sure the boat has its stern facing the wave as we're lifted up, we can't afford to have the waves capsizing us from the side."

Geoffrey was upset by my mutinous retort but he knew that taking down the jib was too perilous a task. He was frightened; he had never been is such a bad storm in twelve years of sailing and he wanted to make the ship as safe as he could but in this case it was impossible. Needing me to help him steer, he decided against sacrificing me. Instead, trying to hide the fear in his eyes, he looked ahead. I was ready to take the tiller, so I stood up properly and moved next to him.

"Okay," I said.

"Will you keep us steady while I'm gone?"

"No problem."

I had to reassure him. Geoffrey was an experienced sailor, more than a decade in dinghies and well over a decade on the open seas. If he was worried then the situation had to be bad.

I grabbed the tiller, firmly and looked over my shoulder as a wave picked us up and dropped us into the swell, the next wave came from a different angle and I steered the boats stern to face it dead on. It scooped us up, and I felt my stomach lurch, as we rose high above the dip.
"It's hard work," explained Geoffrey. "The waves are coming from behind, but at different angles and from different directions all the time. I've never seen a sea like this. Steer her so that the stern faces the incoming wave. Don't whatever you do allow the wave to break over our side or we've had it."
"Got it," I interjected needlessly.
"As we ride down the wave; keep the bow following in the same direction as the wave. When you reach the depression of the wave, look around to see the direction of the next wave that will carry us up. You want to make sure the wave is directly behind you or near as damn it."
He handed me the tiller and headed for the hatch. I appreciated the trust he placed in me, I was a novice and I held all our lives in my two hands. Two hands were needed, the turbulent seas were like a bog and the tiller felt was if it was stuck in molasses. The metal rudder dragged in the currents and the wooden handle in my hands was barely responsive.
"Okay, you check on the jackets and see how the girls are," I called after him.
He slid open the hatch cover and looked down into the cabin, turned his rain-lashed face towards me, his features contorted by a look of disgust and he shouted above the noise, "They're still spewing on their bunks"
With that sympathetic observation, he opened the double doors and disappeared below. I was already breathless and shaking, only a few minutes before joining Bill in the cockpit, I had been taking down the main sail. I had to crawl over the cabin roof that seemed to buck beneath me like a wild beast.
Once I had almost been claimed by the sea as a wave crashed over the deck but I had been saved by firmly holding onto the gunwales which ran along the roof. Winching down the mainsail had been arduous work, kneeling on the roof, clinging with one arm onto the mast as I slowly released the teeth of the winch. As the rope slackened, I clumsily tried to furl the sail with my free hand but it had become a dripping, slippery, nylon mass.
Every few minutes I would have to change arms so that I could rest my tired muscles. The deck and roof moved underneath me and the mast provided my only anchor. I slowly lowered the halyard. It had to be a slow process, if I let the sail down in one go it would have spread over the deck forming a slippery mess that would have left me stranded and exposed for the rest of the voyage.
Even with my inexperience I knew the dangers of slipping over wet sails when your only form of purchase was the boom. If the boom was covered in sail too it would be even harder to stay attached to the boat. All it needed was one slip, a sudden unsettling wave and I would be over the side. I would have had no chance even with a life jacket; hypothermia would claim me in a few hours. There was no way a boat our assize would be able to turn around in such a storm. The fact that the boat only possessed two children's life jackets, and they had been given to the rest of the crew, made me even more cautious.
There was the alternative of slipping down through the bow hatch but that would mean struggling past the flapping jib and going further forward than was safe. I was not sure I would make it over the slippery deck with nothing to hold onto and then I would have to struggle with the two heavy metal clips that secured the hatch.
Deciding not to make the task more difficult than it was, I took my time to slowly and

steadily release and wrap the sail around the boom as best I could. I had enough loops of rope to do the job but my stowing away was far from perfect. Furling a sail of that size would take two men, perhaps three, to do it properly. One man with one arm could make a real mess of it and I had but I was cheered by the knowledge that the boat would not be capsized by the main sail.

That immediate danger had been dealt with. There were many stories of boats keeling over, pushed by the their canvas, a wave slops over the deck into the cockpit, the water disturbs the balance of the boat, another wave crashes over, slopping into the cockpit, the sail helps the boat to topple over, water fills the boat and the crew and boat are lost. The jib was just an annoyance, it flapped loosely but noisily up ahead but it posed no danger. There was no way I would go forward again.

Geoffrey came up again as we rode the incline of another wave, an escalator ride to the top and a steel slide down to the bottom; the ascent took two thirds of the time, the descent one third. The sea underneath swelled up like a balloon and then deflected. We never knew on which side of the wave we would come down, or which part would fall away beneath us, sending us sliding into another cavity in the sea.

"There are only two life-jackets," complained Geoffrey. "Unfortunately, they're both for children."

He stood close to me as he relayed this piece of cheering news. That was it, divine intervention, we were being punished for taking those two Germans for a day's sailing. We had torn those two unfortunates from the land and deposited them amongst the waves. It was a heinous crime to take on responsibility for others when we were not even able to take it on for ourselves. It was therefore fitting that the transgression of decency should be punished and a fitting sentence was death. I accepted it quite casually. Fishermen died in storms, sailors died at sea. The Captain was a dirty old leech and I had been complicit and curious. We deserved to drown. It was the hitch hikers that I felt sorry for; I had never heard tell of a hitch-hiker lost at sea.

"There's Vilamoura," Geoffrey cried without a hint of relief.

I was puzzled, after all that was destination, yet he did not seem pleased. I could see him pointing to one o'clock off the starboard bow. A wave took us down as my gaze followed his finger and, for a few seconds, all I could see was a mountain of water, its shiny slopes blue, black, marbled with white foam. Then we rose to meet the sky and, through the haze of cloud, I could make out what looked lie a shoreline sitting on the horizon and what looked like a white mass which I took to be the marina due to a dim green and red light at it entrance.

"Thank God, we've almost made it," I sighed.

I was relieved, ignorant and relieved.

"There's no way we can turn the boat in this storm, if we start heading north, we'll be rolled over. Vilamoura is north east, we can't cut across these waves we'd be capsized straight away."

Vilamoura had been at one o'clock a few minutes ago but I looked at the compass, down by my feet, for a second and saw that what he said was true. We were moving north by north west at an alarming speed. We were surfing in record time, it would be impossible to turn the boat; it was like missing the junction on a motorway, only this motorway was a dangerous cauldron of activity. I looked over my shoulder to deal with a few more waves; one came from the right, the next to from the left. I concentrated on prising the stern into the swell so that we could ride over, and not be swept under, the wave. Looking out to my right, I glanced at Vilamoura: the harbour, the refuge, the haven, solid, firm, land. It had suddenly moved to three o'clock. It was

difficult to control my disappointment and anger. This so-called 'experienced' sailor had overshot the port. My thoughts were less than charitable towards my skipper and fellow crewman.
"Brilliant, my brother sends me to get sailing experience and we end up in Sagres," I complained loudly.
My facetious remark fell on deaf ears. Maybe Geoffrey thought I was trying to make light of the situation, or perhaps he was just incredibly thick skinned.
"There is another port we could head for, by which time the storm should have dissipated."
"Great, where is it?" I asked full of hope.
"It's near Albufeira, about three hours away," he replied. "We've been travelling for almost an hour now."
Geoffrey looked at his professional-style mariner's watch: stainless steel, three dials, five hands, luminous characters and digits.
"The fastest time from Olhao to Vilamoura in a race was two hours; we've done it in less than half that time. The fastest time from Vilamoura to Portimao was eight hours; we should make Albufeira in four."
Hearing about racing records failed to reassure me. Yes, we were going as fast as a small speed boat, but the spray and lurching of the boat constantly reminded me that we had to survive for those four hours. It was exhausting; wrenching the tiller with both arms, turning my head to line up the boat, twisting my body as we came down the wave to see which direction the next wave would come from. The need to be alert and the adrenaline pumping stopped me from feeling tired. The need for survival gave me strength.
"Okay, it sounds like a good plan," I agreed.
"I'm just going down below to chart our course," he informed me before dancing by the hatch and disappearing into the depths of the boat, battening down the hatches vas he went.
I wanted to be warm and dry, on a beach, just like anyone else on the Algarve in April. I distrusted the captain after he had overshot our destination. Was he really that good? I wondered. We had planned for a three hour cruise and there was nothing on board. Olhao had limited provisions and limited fresh water and that was the reason why we had wanted to go to Vilamoura to stock up on provisions. We were the least well-equipped boat out to sea that day. We only had one flare, the safety harness had gone missing, and there were only two tiny lifejackets, no food and little water. Only two members of the crew were able to sail the boat. I wondered what would happen if we were all pitched into the ocean.
The black silhouettes of tankers could be clearly seen as we neared the shipping lanes but only sporadically when we were heaved up onto the wave top. They disappeared on our descent. The force of the storm was pushing us further into one of the busiest shipping lanes in the world. I was not overly worried at this prospect.
"When your numbers up, your numbers up, it's a simple as that." I told myself repeatedly.
There were obviously lots of things I wanted to do; perhaps we would survive this ordeal by water. Everyone who has sailed in these parts had heard of some boat or other run over by a tanker or worse and less quick, the wake from one of their large propellers capsizing a vessel, once, it was rumoured swamping a catamaran. We had only one hull and the buoyancy of steel was far less superior to the wood or fibreglass of other vessels so we were twice as vulnerable.

I could imagine the scene as I held the tiller, four adults tearing at two children's life-jackets as gallons of water poured on board, pushing the boat under. I imagined the boat shipping water and a furious fight to pump the bilges, followed by the sudden sinking of the boat. All we needed to make us less able to survive was the extra weight of water. Already the gunwales were being lapped by the choppy water that moved around our hull.

These small waves, which escorted us through the peaks, and troughs, were a real danger. Too much water over the side and into the cockpit would result in us sitting lower in the water, more water on board would make the boat heavier and this in turn would make the rudder even stiffer or perhaps impossible to move. A rogue wave would finish the job.

Danger is a funny thing – you either remain calm and accept whatever hand you are given and deal with each situation as it arises, or you panic – The only really experienced sailor on board, Geoffrey, our esteemed skipper seemed to be closer to the latter of these options. I was veering towards the former, but ignorance is bliss. I reasoned that we had been on the same course for a long time and nothing adverse had happened. The jib was still up but so were we, the situation seemed fairly stable. Once our vessel was submerged, that was the time to worry. Naturally, we would not last long in the water, hypothermia is such an efficient killer, but it had not come to that. I comforted myself with the thought that we could all abandon ship, jump in the little rowing boat that acted as the yacht's tender and we could be safe for a few days, starvation would be our only concern. I soon realised that such a small boat would be overturned in such high seas and then I remembered that we had leant the tender to someone else in Olhao so even that was not an option.

Therefore it really was a case of sink and swim. Would I be able to fight off and overcome the rest of the crew and snatch the two small life preservers, using them as water wings, or would I be a gentleman and offer the life jackets to the landlubbers who had not envisaged such a situation and did not deserve to be here? That was the question. There's the rub, what do you d when the instincts of survival cuts in, a real situation where death stares you in the face and you want to survive? Do you die a hero's death or live the life of a villain?

Were these hikers responsible by being stupid enough to come with us? Had they been bullied into joining us, did that make them more, or less, culpable? Should that be punished? Was the Captain responsible, and therefore did he deserve to go down with his ill-equipped ship. Could I live with myself, knowing that I had survived knowing that I only achieved my survival by taking the lives of others? I felt sure that I would be noble. The girls were safe unless the Captain decided to bludgeon all of us to death with a windlass handle and make off with both buoyancy aids. It was with great relief that I realised that 'Captain Instability' was as capable of doing that as I was of getting us safely into any harbour.

His idea was to see if the storm eased and then bolt for port. I supported this course of action despite the fact that the storm seemed to be worsening, we were getting further from land and we were only a few hours into the bad weather. I knew storms could last for days and they generally got worse before they got better but I had to cling to some hope. I had time to think as I wrenched the rudder from port to starboard, tugging on the tiller as each wave came from an unexpected direction. I challenged myself to appear completely clam. I wondered how long I could keep this subterfuge going as we surfed successfully down another slope on the sea. It was bravado but it was necessary for morale; if I seemed unconcerned and got on with the job in hand, it might reassure and calm our Captain. It might at least give him some respite, a chance

to think of solutions rather than imagine the appalling scenarios that I had been conjuring up.
My own equipment was astonishingly in appropriate too. I needed a lifejacket, a sou'wester, full oilskins, and a decent harness with a life belt in order to feel secure. Instead all I had was my belief that we would survive with or without the help of our skittish skipper.
My mind ran from concern for the poor hikers, to the next big wave and then to the worry about whether the Captain was up to the task. The poor, young teenagers, hitch-hiking through Europe, had been asked if they would like a day's sailing. They had refused at first but had relented after Geoffrey's pestering.
It was difficult to refuse him. Perhaps they thought it would be an experience that they would never forget. How right they were, if we lived, then we could all report one of the most life-threatening experiences that anyone could endure. If we sank and subsequently drowned, we could be assured of being immortalised through one of the stories told about sailors in Portugal.
I wondered why I had ever contemplated a life at sea with its brine dampness and lack of predictability. I had read 'Moby Dick' and I knew about the deprivation of Cook and Nelson on their voyages. Even in fair weather it was uncomfortable, cold, damp and windy most of the time with a barely warm sun in the sky and the cold ocean below chilling everything. This storm was something else altogether, mental concentration along with physical strength would save us.
Our minds had to focus on the direction of the next wave and we needed brawn to steer the boat into the right path. It was an exhilarating and eerie feeling, sliding down those massive waves. Would we take on water at the bottom, could we predict the next roll of the waves? As we came up again would we be tossed about by a freak wave and rolled onto our side?
I was cold and thirsty. In this rough sea making a cup of coffee could be fatal. If the storm drove us further out to sea we would either starve or die of hypothermia, alternatively we might be run over by an oil tanker unable to see us in the foul weather. I had always sailed in warm climes to avoid such a situation; my sailing in England had been limited to dinghy sailing in Portsmouth harbour.
Generally, I had sailed in Greece, a land locked island hop, away from international shipping. I had only ever been in one bad rainstorm, although I had heard tell of terrible storms in the Aegean and Adriatic and I had read enough Greek Mythology to be aware of the rough time the Argonauts had experienced, I naively assumed that these were winter storms. (I had travelled so little in spring that I had expected sunshine all the way from May to June, excepting the odd rain shower.
In 1978 I had been in Canada for the six weeks of the summer holiday and it only rained twice and that had been at night. Two years before that England and the rest of Europe had a summer-long heat wave, which had started at the end of May.
There was a certain realism in my expectations, showers could be encountered, the odd chill wind, but a full-blown storm, from Force Eight to Force Ten, simply was not no my agenda and the shock was almost numbing. I could have expected bad weather if I had been sailing in February or September, if it were the Bay of Biscay or anywhere else in the north Atlantic but we were close to the Mediterranean. If we had could have turned back we would have headed due south, turned left at the Rock of Gibraltar and the next stop would have been Africa with its deserts and tropical weather.
My mother had taken us to Mojacar near Alicante; we had seen the deserts where they filmed the "Spaghetti Westerns" with Enio Moriconi's haunting music. The area we

were in was not a place I associated with bad weather, yet we were in a terrible storm. The rain never stopped, its persistence jarred my nerves and yet it felt surprisingly warm compared to the cold wind and the cold spray.

The low temperature surprised me most; it seemed to be only two or three degrees above freezing. The wind cut through everything. My hands and face were raw from the spray of icy water and the lash of cold air from the wind. My skin tingled. I think that my teeth might have chattered if it were not for the determined grimace that I wore. I had been at the tiller for over an hour when I was relieved to hear Geoffrey's voice bellowing from below. He surfaced a few minutes later.

"I've bedded down our guests; I should go below for a while and get dry and warm if I were you," he said nonchalantly.

"Thanks, I will," I replied weakly.

"You've done a really good job, well done," said Geoffrey, looking me in the eye. Suddenly all the respect I had for him returned. It was amazing how appreciation altered my perception of him.

"Thanks," I murmured.

It was a comic sight, the two of us changing places; we danced around each other our legs firmly apart to keep our balance more fully. For the first time that day, I realised that the metal deck was in three inches of water and my shoes and feet were soaked. Geoffrey came towards me, slipping and sliding on the white-painted metal sheet that formed the floor. It was totally impractical and unsuited for wet sailing. I handed him the tiller, gingerly, as we rode up a wave. I had waited until our stern was aligned with the up-coming wave before beckoning him forward from the cabin hatch. He took the tiller and looked nervously over the cabin roof, down the wave, as we slid along the water.

The waves had got even larger. I had become immune to them, adjusted to their gradual change, he had not. I sat next to him for a while and watched him look over his shoulder to line up the boat's stern to a wave which was coming from a completely different yet again. We rode up it and down and into the dip and I watched him take the next wave. The rain poured off his oilskins and I noticed with envy that he was wearing gloves. I rubbed my red sore hands together between my knees and felt the dampness of the rain weigh heavily on my clothes.

"Are you all right?" I asked him.

"Fine, go below," he ordered.

"Are you sure?"

He nodded with little confidence but I needed to be warm, so I danced across the wet floor as if it was a paddling pool, hanging on to anything I could get a purchase on: the seat, the various ropes and stays, the boom, all the paraphernalia of sailing, now made redundant as wave not wind pushed us on. I reached the cabin and wrestled with the hatch and cabin doors, climbed down the steps, closed up the cabin behind me and charged straight into the master cabin.

I saw two towels and grabbed one to dry my hair. I walked unsteadily back, past the two moaning bodies covered in sleeping bags. I felt the roll of the boat below deck. I felt sure that I would fall on one of them and compound their suffering by crushing them. They were most probably wondering, between groans, what had possessed them to go off with two strangers on a voyage which increasingly looked like it would end in disaster.

I, too, wondered what I was doing. I had left my home comforts to sail with my brother on his wooden yacht and, after a series of mishaps, he had persuaded me to get some sailing experience with another skipper. So that was why I was in the storm

to end all storms. I was wet and tired, being jostled around the Atlantic by the worst storm imaginable while my brother lounged in a safe harbour, which may not even have rain let alone a gale.
Added to the obvious discomfiture of being in a storm, I was cold and hungry too and that did not take account of the hopelessness of being driven by an unrelenting sea, the bucking and swaying of the boat, the sight of the two casualties to seasickness, worming around on the bunks and my utter lack of faith in the skipper.
Being naïve, I had assumed that the weather on the Algarve would be mild, not tempestuous, and I had packed accordingly. It had been perfect sunshine when we left the island off Olhao. I did not mind just being cold, I did not mind just being soaked but being both together was miserable. I reasoned that I should have stayed at home in England; too late for that. I should have never left "Waterwitch", my brother's boat and his care; too late for that too. It slowly dawned on me that it was too late for anything. We capsized, sank, starved or we survived. I favoured the latter option but the elements seemed to favour one of the former scenarios.
Despite my unsteady gait, I managed to locate my overnight bag amongst the debris and ignoring the groans of the others, I made my way back into the main cabin. The skin was wet but the lining was dry, I had bought a good quality sailing bag, fortunately and I was rewarded with dry clothes. The walk back to the cabin with the added weight of the bag was even slower than before and my legs were bent like a horse-rider straddling a saddle to give me stability. I was impressed that I had managed to avoid the contents of the now upturned bowls which had been used to accept the hitch hikers' vomit.
Drying myself was a problem, I did not want to get the bed wet as it was the only dry part of the boat. Fortunately the forward hatch had been closed before we set sail, most boats leave harbour with the hatches open to air out the dampness and dew from the previous night.
The problem was not so much staying upright as I peeled off the layers, the boat was still acting like a car on a roller coaster, added to that the feeling of motion in the depths of the vessel was increased and I was beginning to feel seasick. The smell of vomit from the heads and from the upended bowls did not help matters. I cursed myself for ever believing that sailing would be fun. I cursed my brother for allowing me to go off with a relative stranger and I cursed Geoffrey for not reading the forecast at Olhao before ploughing into the Atlantic.
My brother's words rang in my ears:
"Go and get some experience, we have ac day or two before Patrick joins us. We haven't done much sailing, it's a marvellous opportunity."
It was a marvellous opportunity, a marvellous opportunity to drown. I cursed my eldest brother for his inopportune arrival date, just for good measure. We would have set off south for Cadiz if we did not have to wait for him to fly into Faro.
I was feeling sorry for myself. Geoffrey had never seen seas this bad and nor had I, and nor did I want to see them. Up until that moment, I had thought it was a smart move to spend the summer sailing around the Mediterranean. Even then, I knew that it might not all be plain sailing. Along with the sunshine, there had to be a little rain sometime, I just wished that it had not all come at once. Trapped in a fifty-two foot boat when Portugal is experiencing one of the worst storms in its entire history was not my idea of an ideal holiday. Perhaps it would be better if I started at the very beginning.

Chapter Two

Sail Away, Sail Away

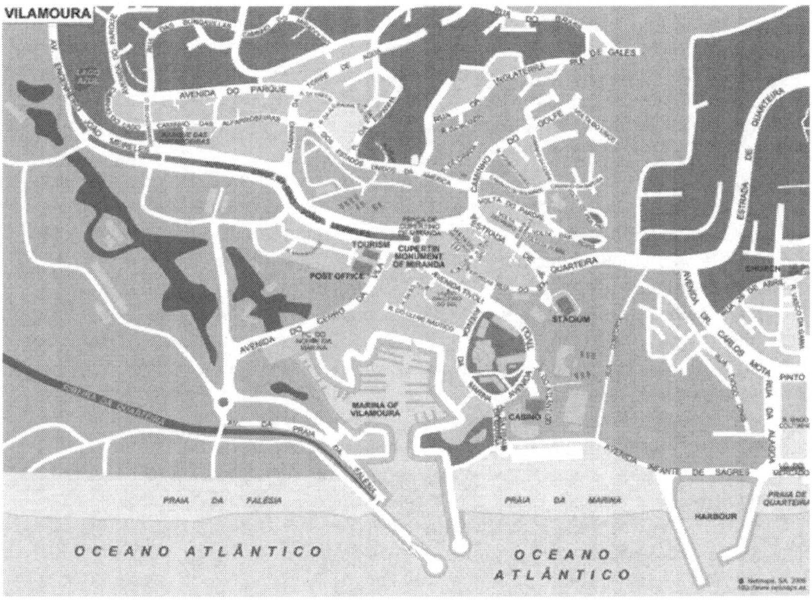

Pristine white walls, symmetrically arranged pontoons, shining white hulls, mirrored masts in blue, calm water; a sun that shone with Mediterranean intensity, that was Vilamoura marina on the Portuguese Algarve. In 1982 the harbour was newly completed, the foundations of the hotel were being sunk into the sea and refugees from Mozambique lived in a shanty town on the beach between the old town and new marina.

Modern cleanliness and newness pervaded the harbour; even the air was clean, fresh and new, a breeze blowing in from off the Atlantic Ocean. Rows of yachts, stainless-steel rigging straining and clicking in the wind, furled white sails, sun-bleached as if they had just been fitted, clean decked to reflect the sun.

We stood, my brother and I, at the white counter in the cool café, our faces and figures reflected in the clear glass of the mirror behind the bar and on the wall behind us. We had been served by an unhappy looking Portuguese girl in a pressed white shirt and black skirt to her knees, a starched apron around her waist. She had not responded to our cheery greeting of “Boom dia”. It did not look like it was a good day for her. Whether her sad expression was due to her genetic make-up or her general disposition, it was hard to tell.

It made me feel perhaps that the Portuguese were not as friendly or relaxed as the Spanish people I had come across. Certainly the customs men who had insisted on our unpacking all of our cases when we had landed at Faro airport the previous evening

seemed officious and cold but what government official does not. That and the miserable attitude of the girl who served us coffee coloured my judgment.
The whole place seemed soulless and unwelcoming. The café we used was in the middle of a row of white-washed buildings, which lined the east side of the harbour. Large, plate glass windows formed black mirrors against the white and the apartments above had their wooden white shutters closed; their owners absent at this time of year, May was not a busy month for tourists.
The tiled floor on which we stood still gave off the smell of bleach; the counter and serving area were of a showroom standard, cutlery, coffee machine, china plates and saucers, all of course white, and glasses polished to perfection. There were no stools or chairs; you were not expected to stay. It was just a corridor really. Even on the veranda outside there were no plastic chairs and tables, they had not arrived as yet. I felt sure that when they did, they would be white.
I sipped my warm cafe "Galao" from the tall, thick glass. An elongated spoon stood in it to prevent the glass from cracking with the heat. I dared not remove it and put it on the spotless saucer, particularly as the coffee had been poured so efficiently without spilling a drop. "Galao" is delicious, one part espresso coffee, strong and dark, a "bica" in Portuguese, to which is added three parts of hot milk. It is a fantastic breakfast tonic. Together with the wonderful custard cake, "Pasteis-de-Nata", it was a breakfast to rival coffee and croissants.
In contrast to the clinical order of the place, Anton and I wore cut off jeans and bright t-shirts, his was yellow, mine was turquoise, it was after all the eighties and bright coloured clothing was acceptable on holiday. Neither of us was in a talkative mood after chatting into the night on our arrival and getting to bed far too late. It was about half past eight and we had not really woken up. After our coffee, we felt restored and Anton outlined the plan for the next few days, which was basically getting "Waterwitch" ship shape and ready to sail.
The coffee had certainly got my gastric juices going and we bought a bag of Portuguese Custard Tarts to eat on our way back to the boat. We ate as we walked in the early May sunshine, a warm sea breeze at our backs. There was a sandy dirt road on either side of the complex and on either side was a collection of building site debris, empty cement bags, a collection of bricks, a small hill of coarse builders' sand, plastic buckets which once held whitewash and a few empty paint pots.
Walking along the beach to the old village of Vilamoura, we passed through the shanty-town and for the first time that day I felt that I was back in the real world. The "Favela" consisted of shacks made of wood chipboard or sheets of corrugated iron draped with the flag of Mozambique. The inhabitants were refuges from the African continent; the authorities tolerated them because they had no policy to provide them with anywhere else to go.
No doubt they found work on the various construction sites surrounding the area. I wondered how long they would last on this beach once the development was complete. Everyone was busy washing for the day or cooking breakfast on open fires or small camping gas stoves. They returned our smiles and greetings.
We strode on purposefully towards town to buy our paint. Everyone stared, a continental habit, perhaps at our clothes, we were not dressed fro work or wondering if we were French, German or English. They would never have guessed we were Irish both of us blonde and blue-eyed; my eldest brother had the dark hair and dark eyes, the more common cultural stereo-type.
In town, Anton bought a baguette, a quarter kilo of local cheese that because it smelt suspect had to be good, a jar of apricot jam and a tin of Danish butter. How clever of

the Danish to put butter in a can specifically for sailors. Returning to the boat we breakfasted on the provisions and brewed a pot of tea using tea bags brought with us from home.
There was no kettle, so like the refugees on the beach, we boiled a saucepan of water on the gas flame. That was and would be our kitchen: a small, blue "Calor" gas bottle, about twelve centimetres high, a black knob that controlled the valve and a steel cage of three metal bars on which to rest on which to any pots or pans. I wondered what I was doing there as I munched my jam sandwich, sitting in the cockpit, the sun shining on me.
The truth is I was enjoying having another year off. I had given up a job that I had not enjoyed to help Anton to sail this beautiful boat around the Mediterranean, it was that simple. My brother, Anton, had been in a terrible motorcycle accident, losing one and half inches off one leg. To help his body heal my mother, a doctor, had suggested he go to a warmer climate and he had taken up sailing in the Canary Island. One of his journeys had brought him to Vilamoura on the Portuguese coast.
Whilst the boat he was crewing on was being prepared for charter in the summer, he came across the most beautiful sailing boat that he had ever seen, “Waterwitch”, built in 1937 by Uffa fox, a famous boat builder and marine architect, who had been based in Cowes. The yacht had a very successful racing career but somehow landed up sunk in Gibraltar harbour. A hippie called John salvaged the boat and made it his home, sailing from port, to marina, to harbour, to fishing village and playing his guitar in bars. He had been playing his guitar for ten years along the south west coast of Portugal.
My brother wanted the boat, so he asked John what he would rather be doing, if he had the money. John answered that he would rather be in the Seychelles strumming his guitar there. That was it my brother would make it happen. In return for a single ticket to the Seychelles, via London, Anton took possession of a handmade mahogany, sitka spruce and teak racing yacht, forty three feet and six inches of incredible beauty. There was very little persuasion needed to convince me to help him crew the boat. I handed in my notice, they kindly let me leave with only a week’s notice, and I booked a return flight through Monarch airways to Faro airport, not realising I would be visiting Faro more times than I planned.
The fact that I had very little experience in the sailing filed seemed to matter little to my brother. He had his in-shore and off-shore certificates as a yacht master from the Royal Yachting Association and I had sailed twice in the Greek islands where there are no real tides. I could hardly wait to get going. My sailing days had consisted of dinghy sailing in Portsmouth harbour with the CCF (Combined Cadet Force) at school and two holidays with the YHA. The first trip, off the west coat and in the Adriatic, sailing from Paxos to Levkas, and the second year was sailing in the Aegean taking in islands like Skiathos and Ithaca in the Sporades. The school had arranged the trip, part of a flotilla sailing holiday, a great two weeks of fun at Easter. So good I tried it twice.
There was nothing to do, no tides to worry about, the boat was a “Mirage” twenty four foot, which was small but comfortable, a cruiser with a cooker, shower and soft bunks and cushions in the cockpit. I imagined our boat being bigger would be even more luxurious. I was sharing a flat with a friend from school and the flat had become a focal point for all our friends coming to London, my room would be taken in a shot and I would worry about finding accommodation on my return. The days were getting longer and the evenings were getting lighter as spring arrived and my brother’s girlfriend, Joanna drove us to the airport.

The pan was to work on the boat fro the rest of May, leave the marina on 1st June and meet up in July with Jo and some of her friends on the island of Ibiza. We would stay in the Balearic Islands for the month of July, sail to Sete in the south of France, up through the Rhone, into the canals of France, ending up on the French side of the Channel. From there we would sail to moorings in the Kent area. That was the plan at the beginning of our trip.

We took off from Gatwick in the evening and arrived as the last flight into Faro airport, which had just been redesigned and expanded, all red and yellow, glass and steel. On the flight I had satisfied myself with the view of Faro port and the blue, black sea as we banked to line up with our approach to the runway; my mind was full of feelings of a great adventure about to begin.

The bubble burst when we picked up our holdalls from the baggage carousel. Each of us had an extra bag with equipment and stores needed for the boat. We were eyed suspiciously by the customs officials. Even to this day, I cannot work out what made them search us. Perhaps they feared we were Special Forces unit intent on overthrowing the King of Spain and therefore removing Spain's support for Argentina in the Malvinas, or the Falklands.

Was it our bulging bags, our Irish passports, always a problem with the troubles in the north, or was it the fact that we were tall with light coloured hair, almost Scandinavian looking, in contrast to these Latin types? Weren't Irish generally a similar colouring with dark hair and similar stature? We were not fair skinned either. My brother had been in Canaries of a month and I had spent the previous summer in Spain sunbathing using olive oil and I had been back to Malaga for a top up in February. We had tans. Despite our casual dress of shirts and jeans, we were quite obviously smugglers as far as they were concerned. Maybe they didn't like the look of us or maybe they just didn't like their jobs.

We declared everything but the bored customs men were not satisfied that we had done so. I might have been suspicious of us; we did look exceptionally fit, like soldiers and we were carrying a lot of excess baggage and we did not fit the profile, why would two Irishmen look like Vikings. Weren't all Irish carrying bags packing Semtex, the IRA had spoiled the reputation of Irish people since the early seventies. A decade later their reputation preceded them.

I felt like using Oscar Wilde's words when he arrived in America, "I have nothing to declare but my genius." Instead, I looked suitably fed up, they looked far too mean and they were armed which always makes me uncomfortable and terribly polite. They had nothing else to do, it was the end of a long and tedious day for them and they had a job to do. Anyone who looked suspicious needed to be challenged; it was the way it was. We were tired and anxious to get to the boat so it was inconvenient but we knew they had a job to do.

It was about nine thirty, I didn't blame them, but unpacking and re-packing our bags was a difficult and tiring experience. The bags had been packed with such great care and precision that trying to fit everything back into the bags, once it had been inspected, proved very trying. We had brought over an awful lot: filler powder, special paints, special finishes, and varnishes, parts for the engine that in fact might have formed part of a weapon, a new sail and canned goods. All of it had been brought out for inspection, and then thrown in a heap by our bags. It was up to us to put everything back in we could. They scattered our belongings over the tables and all we could do was look on and try to replace everything as best we could, it was not the most auspicious arrival in Portugal.

We found a cab outside; we were one of the last few people to leave the airport from our flight. Anton warned me that the taxi driver's driving could be dangerous. The driver must have been in a hurry to get home, making this the last job of the evening. Sitting in the back of the car, I was worried that it might be his final job and our last ride ever. Despite the driver, who dropped us off at the corner of the yacht pool, we arrived safely. All Portuguese drivers in those days thought they could drive like the Brazilian racer Emerson Fittipaldi. There was a three-lane freeway outside the airport, the EN125 and we moved rapidly along the road despite and because of the traffic lights, each light had to be passed before it changed red. Vilamoura was twenty nine kilometres west of Faro so we were not kept in the car too long. Anton had said it would take about twenty five minutes, we made it in fifteen.

Carrying the heavy bags along the pontoons was no joy; I was hoping that "Waterwitch" was nearby, given that the taxi driver would not go onto the dirt track road that led to the pontoon. Alas, it was one of the furthest away. Anton pointed it out to me in the darkness, floodlit by the marina lights. My heart sank, even under the artificial glow of floodlights, it was clear that the boat needed an awful lot of work to make it seaworthy.

When we reached the boat, he pulled back the tarpaulin from over the cockpit and unlocked the hatch, sliding back the roof and lifting out the door, which he placed to one side before reaching up to the pontoon so I could pass the four bags down to him. It was disconcerting to notice that the gunwales were less than a metre above the water. I also noticed that most of the forty six foot of the boat was out of the water, the yacht was formed into two tapered ends, like an old-fashioned cigar. The shape was great for streamlining and racing, equal to an aeroplane but did not leave much room for living space.

Finally, after some swearing the bags were stowed. Inside the cabin, neither of us could stand properly as it was only a metre and half high and we both stood at over two metres, so we sat down quickly in the cramped, damp cabin. Anton wedged himself onto a bunk and offered me a place beside me.

"This is the lounge," he grandly announced.

"Lounge, more like crawl," I replied.

We had left England on 8th May. Rising early, our first task on Sunday was to unload the boat and sort through the equipment, making sure there was a place for everything and everything was in place. It was not a day of rest but in the evening we had barbecued pork at a restaurant called the "Cabana". It was cheap and cheerful, with long bench seats and long refectory-style tables, just like being back at school but the food was superb.

On Monday we took the cockpit apart, sanded it down by hand and sorted and stored the rest of the equipment. If that sounds repetitive, it was. Supper was at the Ritz, the ironic name given to the local transport café by English yachts-people. Swordfish was on the menu, great fish steaks that were fat and succulent. On Tuesday we painted the cockpit and sorted through more equipment. Supper was at the Mayflower, the squid was delicious.

I lived for eating; it was the highlight of a hard day. The name Mayflower conjured up the Puritans and I was sure that they set sail promptly; I was becoming more convinced that we would not. The next day we tidied up the cabin, painted some more and sorted more equipment although by this stage it could have been the same sorted for a second time.

We spent a week sanding down the hull and deck, filling gaps in the timbers and generally patching up a boat that had been neglected for a decade. Eventually,

Waterwitch would be smooth enough for a coat of wood primer and then would be painted white. It was unpleasant work without shelter.
The daily ritual consisted of having a shower in the marina bathing block, then breakfast, followed by smothering our skins in suntan lotion which made our hands greasy. This made holding the sandpaper awkward and we sweated in the heat. Working in hot conditions, dripping oil running off your body was not much fun but finally we were ready to apply the paint. This was even less enjoyable, but progress had been made. We could abandon the sun tan oil at this stage because we had built up such a solid base tan. Besides, it was so annoying being greasy all day.
Despite the fact that this boat looked as if she would never leave harbour. I remained hopeful that one day, I would sail again. After all this was a sailing holiday. Supper became a hunt for variation. We had swordfish at the "Ritz", octopus at the "Cabana", you get the idea. Three restaurants, a limited menu and still our sails remained firmly furled.
Sailing involved moving to new places, variety of locations, new cultures, new regional variations, that sort of thing. I was so familiar with Vilamoura, the transport café to the west, the "Cabana" to the east up the hill in the old town and the Mayflower in the harbour near to our morning coffee corridor, that I could have made it to any of these restaurants blindfolded. Also, I was working hard, not as a crew member, but as a restorer. For this reason I started to become a little resentful. I just wanted to get going.
It was eleven o'clock and yet the heat from the sun was oppressive, certainly not conducive to working out of the shade. The bright sun was painful to look at and the heat generated by it had warmed everything: paint tins, skins, stone pavement, and white deck. A sweat had already formed on my brow and I was aware of a clammy feeling under my armpits. It was one of those skies that look pale and glow blue, which everyone associates with summer in southern Europe. For some strange reason Anton was already writing the log book, which I thought was a diary kept only when we were at sea. Apparently it was necessary to keep a good watch of things in harbour too. He was in fact noting what provisions we needed. What materials had been bought and what further equipment or items that we needed.
As I slapped another coat of paint on yesterday's work, it struck me that this religious half hour every day allowed my brother time off from manual work. I stood up in the dinghy with the hot sun on my back. I had given up wearing my t-shirt as it just made me hotter. While keeping my balance on the water and bending to smear more paint onto my brush, I carefully brushed the primer onto the side of the boat, concentrating on each brush stroke; I heard the lemonade bottle being pulled from the water followed by two stumpy bottles of "Sagres" beer. I pretended not to have heard the making of the first drink of the day. I was hungry; all I had was a glass of "Galao" and a custard tart because due to time constraints we had abandoned our early perambulations into town to get breakfast. Instead we saved ourselves for our evening meal of roast quails at the truckers' café or chicken barbecued over charcoal at the "Cabana".
Shopping for food in the evening, we would pick up our bread and cheese for the following day from the shops as they were closing. If we didn't make it to town before the bread shops shut, we negotiated for bread from the restaurant and eked out our supply of cheese. We had jam on board in case we were not cautious enough with our cheese rations. It was important that we tried to keep to our schedule.
The possibility of spending the whole summer working on the boat was a real one. We therefore elected to get "Waterwitch" seaworthy and nothing more. This,

inevitably, involved working long hours in the hot sunshine, we were lucky not to get sun stroke. The skin on my shoulders and back was peeling and I felt that if I didn't have a drink of any kind soon, then my throat would begin to peel also. Just as I was about to curse my brother; he arrived with a shandy. Suddenly, life seemed better and I drank slowly, savouring the drink almost feeling like I was on holiday.

Dealing with bureaucracy is the mist frustrating of clerical tasks and leaving Vilamoura was the most frustrating of bureaucratic nightmares. Anton remained calm but I could not, I was bored of menial work and painting. I could have got a job painting in London, making money instead of spending it. I wanted to be sailing. Despite my itchy feet, I put on a brave face, the officials were armed. Still I felt like throttling them before they could draw their pistols. I found the soulless marina with its hollow clinical feel a strange place; it was like being in a limbo, it felt like we had arrived somewhere just after the party and everyone had gone.

We languished in the harbour, only connecting with real people only in the shanty town and when we went out each evening, but even this treat was beginning to pall. Once you have had chicken and fish, there was nothing else on the menu. The novelty of eating on benches with charcoal and flagons of wine stacked up against the walls wore off very quickly.

You could not choose who to sit next to on the benches and Portuguese is a difficult language to master. We were too exhausted to talk much so scintillating conversation was off the menu. Eating in meal in silence is like listening to pop music without the drum beat or an orchestra without piano and violin, it just does not sound right.

Our rare visits to the transport café where we ate quails were worthwhile and satisfying but it was deemed too far to walk just for decent food. The walk was over rough roads, pitted by grooves made by the huge six wheel and eight wheel construction trucks, it was a horrendous hike. The Victorians used to say: "After lunch rest a while, after supper walk a mile", but two miles was excessive. A four mile round trip became a hardship after a full day of work.

Finally, after much bureaucratic wrangling, filling of forms and photocopying documents, we got clearance to leave harbour. Our next visit to the local store was to be our last, so we went to the bank, took out some money and bought plenty of honey. With our wads of "Escudos", we also bought bread, wine and a noxious local spirit which came in the same type of bottle as the paraffin we had bought earlier. There was no electricity on board so we had to use hurricane lamps, which we filled with paraffin from what looked like stretched, clear wine bottles with a plastic cap stopper. These we had bought by the crate load.

The only other items we could possible take were cheese and beer as we lacked a fridge, the sea would cool our drinks. We had to prioritise, butter would melt and become rancid. "Waterwitch" travelled lightly and swiftly. Our range was to be counted in days, three days at sea, at the most, and then we would have to find a harbour and replenish our stores.

Fresh water was supplied by a fifty litre Jerry can filled form the harbour tap which the harbour master charged for. Coffee and tea bags had been bought from home with a single jar of English apricot jam, heavy on the sugar, light on the fruit. That was that as far as home comforts were concerned. You cannot beat English tea even though my mother insisted that tea bags contained the dust from real tea, the shaving from the floor as she called them. She had been bought up on loose leaf tea and strainers, which was a little too genteel for our brand of sailing.

The purser on a boat takes care of the stores and Anton made sure that he was the best purser that "Waterwitch" could have. We had bought a bottle of paraffin and a bottle

of wine a day. They sat in a plastic crate stowed in the depth of the cockpit, which was open above and below and therefore we stored items behind it and on both sides cramming goods right up against the skin of the hull. If you squatted down in the cockpit you could see the ribs of the boat on either side, the tapering stern became a cave, which housed oars, sails, buckets filled with paint pots and boathooks.
We had added a crate of beer to the two crates already there and we had bought litre bottles of lemonade. It was rare that we would drink alcohol on its own because in the heat the effects of alcohol are concentrated. The wine we bought was so cheap and rough that it needed lemonade to make it palatable and the beer came in quarter litre stumpy bottles, which made a decent shandy for two in our tin tea cups. I think those cups were part of the original nineteen-thirty-seven inventory.
Our morning fees paid on Thursday 20th May, we were ready to leave. Twelve days after our arrival, I had insisted we go. Preparing for departure involved more sorting through, the paint tins and brushes had to be stowed carefully just in case we had time, at a later date, to finish the job.
"Waterwitch" looked white and right on one side and like a camouflaged First World War cruise on the other. I counted three shades of undercoat and I could not even attempt to count the smears of filler that broke up the outline of that particular side. It was a truly disruptive pattern. We set sail on the ebbing tide, five days after the originally agreed departure date.
There was alight wind and so full of a mixture of relief and trepidation we goose-winged past the customs men who waved enthusiastically as we passed. I wanted to harangue them or say something rude but as we sailed past them at two knots, roughly one and a half miles per hour, it would have looked faintly ridiculous. How uptight and urbanised, I still was. After our ordeals, I became the most relaxed and grateful person on earth.
Once out into the ocean, the wind picked up and we sailed gently and majestically into the open sea. Our mainsail was pushed forward to a right angles to the boat to catch the wind on one side and on the other side we had hoisted a spinnaker a large, light, balloon-shaped sail set forward of the mainsail when running before the wind. Finally, we were sailing, even if it was at three knots. It was an ideal time for Anton to acquaint me with the boat. I tried to show him my knowledge gained from a basic Royal Yacht Association course which I had to attend at school in order to go dinghy sailing in Portsmouth harbour.
It was time to take down the spinnaker that we had used to goose-wing out of harbour and put up a racing jib instead. We released the lines that held the spinnaker in place and let "Waterwitch" drift powered by the mainsail which Anton had lashed to the tiller bar. Then we moved forward to the foresail to winch down the flapping spinnaker. I stood by the forestay, which was the wire that supported the mast and was part of the standing rigging
"So, you're in charge of the jib, when we've got this down" he said.
"Okay," I agreed. "I'll stow the spinnaker."
"Just unclip it and put it through the hatch and I'll fold it and stow it in the cabin. I'll pass up the jib through the hatch."
"I'll unpack it, pass back the cover to you, and then fasten the jib to the forestay."
"That's great, I like the technical terms. Maybe you're more of a sailor than you've been suggesting."
"I'm just pretending, I'm good on the technicals not very good on the practicals"
"This is a good time to learn."
What next?"

“The hanks, those small clips on the wire of the forestay attach to the eyes on the sail. We call them grommets, which is basically the brass ring in a sail or piece of canvas, some grommets are made of rope instead of brass, they’re just rings for attaching the hanks. Attaching the hanks to the grommets is a bit of a fiddly job but it shouldn’t take too long, the clips of the hanks can get quite stiff with no oil but just make sure the sheets aren’t tangled.”

The sheets were the ropes or lines that control a sail, they were attached to the clew of the jib and they would haul the jib from one side to the other when we changed directions. The clew was the bottom corner of the sail. I had to make sure that the sheets were not coiled because they were hauled in from the cockpit at the aft of the boat, the area near the stern. This gave us our steering and power to turn. The jib was the first piece of canvas that caught the wind when you changed direction, if the ropes or sheets got snagged the boat might lose the wind and just drift.

“Where are the winches to haul in the sheets, by the way?” I asked.

“This is a basic boat. See those brass cylinders on either side of the cockpit, they look like drums. You just wind the rope around them just once, one turn only and you’ll here them click. Draw in the sail until it’s almost taut, you cannot let go of the rope until the sail is as trim as can be, then fasten the rope in the teeth underneath. The drums only move in clockwise direction, so you have to wrap the rope around in a clockwise direction so you can tighten it.”

It seemed simple enough to me.

“Then, I fasten them to the two grips."

Back in the cockpit there were two teardrop-shaped wooden blocks fastened to the gunwales on the inside under the brass cylinders. The grips were parallel to each other and they had teeth on the inside edge to grip even the slipperiest of ropes.

“Only when I’ve bought the boom around,” Anton rightly insisted.

As we talked we took down the spinnaker and attached the jib to the halyard, which was the steel line used for hoisting sails.

The foot of the sail sat in the groove of the metal boom. The mainsail was furled around the boom when not in use. When used it was untied, then fastened by clips to the mainsail halyard, a steel wire that hoisted up the mast by a single rope and pulley. There were two hooks which you wrapped the end of the rope around; one hook faced upwards, the other downward. This encouraged you to fasten the rope or sheet around it in a figure of eight fashion. If the weather was good the sail would be hoisted all the way to the top of the mast, if the weather was gusty, then the sail could be hauled three-quarters or half way down up the mast, this was known as being point reefed. It was all complicated stuff to a landlubber like me.

We hoisted the jib, ensured the sheets were untangled and moved back into the cockpit as the jib flapped about and we continued to sail at a snail’s pace along the shore off Quarteira. As we sat down and Anton hauled in the sheet on the port side, he continued his explanation.

“Running from the mast to the beam, or the sides of the boat, are the shrouds. The beam is really the width of the boat. The shrouds are steel cables that give support to the mast. Similar cables called backstays run to the aft of the boat.”

I was getting to know the parts of a sailing yacht, Anton pointed to the stays which rose from behind the cockpit. The beam was the centre of the boat, its widest point, I had called it the middle once but now I was keen to use the correct title.

“What do the shrouds and backstays do apart from support the mast?” I asked.

"Nothing except that one backstay will provide a line for us to run up the courtesy flag, which we will have to change from Portuguese to Spanish when we reach Spanish waters."
"Are they that strict about it?"
"All countries are, it's maritime law, after all, a sign of respect, just like when we are in England we stand for their National Anthem and we expect visitors to Ireland to stand for our Anthem. When in Rome, does as the Romans do."
"I see."
"I believe it was the British who started it," he continued. "Something to do with territorial waters and who commanded them. If you didn't put up a courtesy flag a British frigate might blow you out of the water. I should think most sailors have forgotten why we do it. We can also hand out our washing on the shrouds which is handy. Even jeans dry out very efficiently after two hours tied to the shrouds, the De Nimes flag."
We both laughed but the lesson was not over. He pointed to the port dead-eyes at the bottom of the port shroud; it was a circular block of wood with an iron band running around its circumference. It was pierced with three holes to feed a lanyard through, each hole looking like an eye.
"The bottom of the shroud is made fast around the upper dead-eye. The lower dead-eye is fastened to the gunwale and cannot be detached. If you pull on the lanyard, the lanyard can be tightened in really bad weather.
"I shouldn't think we'll have any bad weather, so why worry?"
At my comment, my brother looked at me quickly and the away before changing the subject to operation of the mainsail.
"The mainsail works in the same way, but the dead-eyes of that are attached to this steel bar that runs along the front of our sailing bench. That bar is known as the sailing horse."
He pointed to a bar that ran along the front and middle of the bench and which was curved at each end, where the metal disappeared into the wood of the bench. It looked as if it would take a lot to separate the two, perhaps as much as it would to detach the wooden plank that formed the bench which was firmly fastened to the skeleton of the boat.
A compass stood on the outside lip of the stairway into the cabin. We had to be careful to step over it when we went below. The bench with the sailing horse that ran a half a metre across the cockpit was set towards the dead eyes more than towards the cabin. The wooden tiller arm protruded across the top of the sailing horse and ran over the back of the bench disappearing into the cave at the stern where it was attached to the rudder by a metal pole.
The gunwales were made of mahogany but the patina and varnish had faded over time and the wood was now grey and weathered. The backstay shrouds were attached to this wood as were the hanks for the foresail. Outside the gunwales on the sloping deck, on either side, were the brass drums, the windlasses. I was keen to show I understood what I had been told and the finer rudiments of sailing
"So I sit or lean on the bench and steer, pull in the jib, then set the mainsail by pulling on the dead-eyes."
"Pretty much, but don't touch the shrouds, you really do need to know what you are doing with those. Once you decide to turn…"
"Come about."

“Once you decide to change tack, you call out: “Jive, ho,” then turn the tiller, loosen the dead eye and let go of the jib in that order. I know others release the jib rope first, but I don’t. As you come about the boom dead eye will slide along the pole.”
“The sailing horse,” I corrected him.
Anton gave me that strange look again.
“Yes, but you only do that once you have the jib trim, then you can haul in the main sheet. If we are sailing together, the responsibilities will be the same, you’ll handle the jib and I’ll handle the mainsail.”
“That sounds clear to be me; by the way, what is a stanchion?”
“Every wire on this boat had a function, to either strengthen the boat or move it faster in the water, the wires are either standing rigging or running rigging, a stanchion is just an upright support, correct?”
“That’s right, put simply. You’ll get used to all the different ropes and wires in no time. Then the only other two things to worry about are the anchor and the ropes to tie up the boats.”
“We call those ropes painters.”
The odd look appeared on Anton’s face again.
“Yes, sailors call them painters. We have other ropes down below that tie the fenders to the boat.
“The fenders are the rubber buoys or tyres that you see attached to the side of boats to stop the scraping against anything or each other. We only use them when we are moored in a proper dock or berth.”
“Okay, I appreciate you have been sailing before but not in a racing yacht and not on this boat.”
“I understand, truly.”
Can an annoying younger brother say anything more provocative?
“Anything else?” he asked testily.
“Are we going to tack at some stage today?”
“Too little wind, I’m afraid, we’ll have to motor-sail from here. You can take down the jib and stow it, the bag for it is in the forward cabin on my bunk.”
“Aye, aye Skipper”
“Get out the Genoa instead it’s the one in the canvas bag.”
“Got it, Genoa, in canvas cover, what about the red nylon bag with the sailing jib, can we use that instead?”
“Do I have a mutiny on my hands? It’s actually in the blue bag; the storm jib is in the red bag.”
“I see.”
“The racing jib’s no use in this, it won’t help much, it’s not the strength of the wind it’s the direction.”
“Oh, I forgot that, we never worried about that dinghy sailing and we could always motor-sail in Greece.”
“We’ll the British seagull engine that I have is reliable but it’s a bit old and missing a few replacement parts, so I prefer to sail where I can.”
“Is that why we sailed out of Vilamoura? I thought you were just showing off, giving the customs men something to talk about, the Irishman who sailed out of the marina.”
“No, I just wanted to practice sailing out of harbour. Remember, I haven’t done much sailing in her either, I’ve only just bought her and John and I only went out a few times.”
“I cannot believe you bought it for £1,500, you couldn’t get a decent second hand car for that money.”

"The price was the cost of the flight to the Seychelles, £1,200, the three hundred was to get him back to England and give him some cash fro when he was establishing himself. At least *Waterwitch* will be sailing more now, instead of lying in harbour. Go and get that Genoa up."

He released the jib sheets and I sauntered down below to get the bag. I slipped through the hatch, down the cabin steps, all four of them, and through the cabin. The chart table had been folded up and it smelt of new paint and I could hear the water lapping against the skin of the boat. It was dark in the cabin.

I started to feel queasy, for one awful moment, I thought I would be sick. I staggered forward to the front of the boat, climbed onto Anton's bed and instead of collapsing onto his bunk like I wanted to; I lifted the hatch cover up and slid it onto the deck. The air immediately revived me; I was determined not to be seasick on my first day out. I subsequently learnt that, it was common to be ill in the first days of sailing.

I soon found the genoa, all the sails seemed to be in bags arranged around Anton's bunk, they looked like the bags that boxers hit when training or like the old fashioned French pillows or bolsters you used to come across in rural France.

Popping my head out of the forward hatch to judge where to throw the bag, I squatted down again, clasped the big bag around its circumference and with a mighty effort raised the heavy canvas through the lip of the hatch way, against which I rested for a moment. Then pushing it form below, I eased it onto the deck, it was much heavier than it looked. To Anton it must have looked like the launch of a "Trident" missile from a "Polaris" submarine, only in slow motion.

I rested for a moment, then, using my arms as leverage, I eased my self up through the hatch and next to the foresail. As I hauled down the jib, I unclasped the brass fasteners, the hanks on the forestay, from the grommets of the jib. The idea of having grommets and the self closing hanks, that worked like a bulldog clip in the fact that it sprang shut, all seemed like a really clever method of doing things. In reality, the springs on the hanks that allowed you to thread them through the grommets had become stiff with age. I suppose the designers envisaged replacing the hanks every few years but these were terribly stiff, probably being at the bottom of a harbour in Gibraltar had down them no good.

The hanks were brass and as old as the boat but the springs inside them made them snap shut and they were as effective as ever in pinching skin. I had to watch my fingers did not get snagged in them. It was pushing the spring back and getting them open that caused the problem, they shut perfectly well but the catch was difficult to push back.

Chapter Three

The Riddle of the Sands

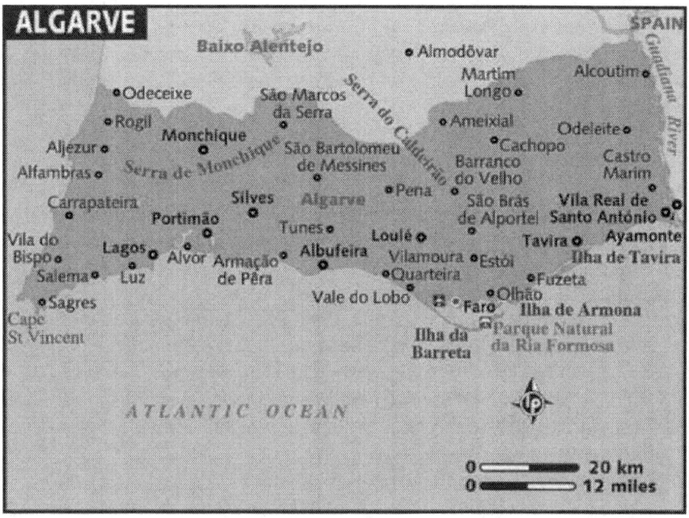

With just the mainsail up, we were going to rely on an outboard motor and the wind in the mainsail to keep us moving. Our outboard motor strapped onto the side of the boat through a complicated arrangement of attachments, brackets, clips and screws. We had a limited amount of petrol but the British Seagull engine was built to pre-war specifications, which guaranteed reliability.

Having unpacked the sail, attached and hoisted it, I moved back into the cockpit, where Anton had pulled all the lines, ropes, and sheets as tight as possible. He immediately gave me control of the tiller and instructed me on which compass bearing to line up the boat to. This would give us the maximum wind on our sails. My brother rummaged around under the stern deck housing, in the cave, while I took the tiller. Eventually he found the small robust engine and strapped it to the port side bracket. Although the engine had very little power, the output produced had a maximum of ten horse power and was designed for boats up to thirty foot long, it could still move our three tons of boat through the water at four knots, a full knot faster than we could sail in that wind. The design had changed little since 1931, so it perfectly resonated with "Waterwitch", both pre-war design triumphs.

When the jib came down our log, a marine pedometer, a line with a spinning propeller, which recorded our rate of passage through the water, actually showed our speed had dropped to two knots so our trusty "Seagull" had effectively doubled our speed. The motor chugged and we smiled at one another. The adventure had finally begun.

It was still light, we put on our sunglasses, we had a full tank of two stroke and we were on a mission. Our plan was clear; to reach Olhao. We kept a weather eye on the sun as it sank slowly behind us in the west behind us. Setting sail from Vilamoura, our yacht would take us into the channel at Faro through the marshes of Parque Natural da Ria Formosa, past the Praia de Faro, skirting the Cabo de Santa Maria and sailing along past the fishing village of Olhao and onto a nearby island to the south-east, a night stop over for many other boats.

We would moor at anchor off the island and join the teeming yacht crews. Apparently the island had a wonderful cabana style bar that served delicious food, great beer and was owned by an old English sea dog who had tales of the Caribbean Sea and stories of adventures in the Mediterranean. From there we would shadow the coast of Spain until we reached the island of Ibiza. All well and good.

However, as we approached Faro, it became clear that unless the wind picked up to eight or nine knots, we would have to rethink our elaborate plans. The drone of the motor and the fading light reminded me of my preconceived ideas of sailing. My perception was of sunlight and speedy progress, a comfortable boat heeled over as it approached the twelve knot mark. I would have to be patient; my dream would have to wait.

The point I was aiming for was a mere speck in the distance and the compass needle remained steady but the reading of numbers around the compass seemed to spin back and forth, first I was ten degrees over the heading, then ten under, it was most disconcerting. It seemed I was weaving and yet the sails did not lose the wind, which would have meant that I had turned too closely into the wind and the sails did not flap which meant that I had moved too far away from the wind. Steering a boat with a wooden tiller behind you and a cabin roof in front of you is difficult work, particularly as the compass bearing seemed to move all the time.

Perhaps we could have walked there more quickly, but we had to take the rough with the smooth, or more especially in our case the rough with the rough. It was early evening by the time we reached the shallows that signified the entrance to Faro. My brother took the helm and he debriefed the crew at five o'clock. Silencing the engine, he announced with triumph that we had enough wind in our sails to make the use of the motor redundant and that we were doing a staggering four knots.

Waiting for me to be suitably impressed led to a long silence. What I wanted to know was: when would we get there? As if wounded by my need to know our ETA, that is estimated time of anchoring, Anton went into various logistics of moving such a small wonderful boat along the coastline. With much reference to her heritage, and lineage, the speed she could and would be able to achieve in the right circumstances, he made it abundantly clear that we were far from these conditions.

"Waterwitch" loved the open seas and felt constrained by the narrow channels and hugging the coast, she needed to tack and jive with a strong offshore wind. With my rudimentary knowledge of sailing, I felt we might consult the chart and see if there was a shortcut. Unfortunately, I was informed that my had not been able to find a chandler in London or in fact the land who possessed the prerequisite navigational map when he had flown back with John and made a list of the equipment needed for his voyage.

They could have been ordered within twenty-one days, by which stage we would be in Ibiza. I found it hard to argue the logic behind this, but as the privileged first mate, I was allowed to look at the Michelin road map which we were to use until we got to Gibraltar and could buy charts of the Mediterranean. In the fading light, I was

fascinated by the coast road that hugged the shoreline; surely it was pleasure to drive along.
The upshot of our conversation was that we would sail through the early evening and with luck and a flowing tide, we would be in Olhao by nine o'clock, anchored and battened down with two beers on the bar by nine-thirty. I had looked over our 'chart' and asked about our average speed, observing silently to myself that this was a hopeful scenario. Sensing my dubiousness, my brother assured me that the wind would be picking up soon, adding that this part of the coast was notorious for its strong winds.
As if to illustrate his point, the flags fluttered as great gusts blew and the sails filled, our speed through the water picking up dramatically. As we tightened and trimmed the ropes and sails, he warned me that one thing we had to watch out for was running aground. It was something we could not afford to do "Waterwitch" had lain at the bottom of the sea when she had run aground before. Armed with this information, I was pleased to be sent forward with a plumb line to take soundings. It was getting chilly and I still wore shorts, but I grabbed my cotton jumper from the cabin as before I moved to the bow. I could feel the hairs on my legs stand up but it was pleasant cooling feeling.
We were in a tight tack and close hauled, so we could not take the best advantage of the new gust. It did seem we were making good progress through the channel until we were overtaken by a lone windsurfer. Skimming pat us over the barely undulating waves, he gave a nonchalant wave and with a pronounced German accent called out a cheery "hello".
My brother took this in good spirit, I was incensed. It was not possible to go faster, it would have necessitated several tacks and the channel was not wide enough to allow us to complete them, so we bobbed along as the wind got fresher and the sun disappeared into the west and ceased to warm wither of us. We were too busy to brew a warming cup of coffee; lashing the tiller and lighting the primus stove was too dangerous with the prospect of hitting a sand bank. If got too close we would have to turn into the wind and steer away from a collision.
I was acutely aware of our two metre keel creeping along underneath us, while I took sounding of two metres fifty, two metres, sixty and two metres, seventy. When we had entered the channel, we were sure that the tide was carrying us along. In fact it was only the wind. The tide was ebbing and the light was fading. Eventually, we made it out into another channel and this allowed Anton to light the hurricane lamps and turned on our navigational lights. There was a pathetic glow from the rusted oil lamps despite the fact that we had trimmed the wick. Black, oily smoke eased up the chimney, clouding the already dirty glass. It would not be possible to read a book from these lights which were meant to warn people of our presence. The small electric lights shone dimly from the mast, on red one green, which would show other boats what direction we were going in, although they would have to be practically on top of us to differentiate between the two colours so weak was their beam.
We started to pick up speed as we had more room in which to turn the boat more easily. Up ahead in the distance, the shimmering lights of Faro could be clearly seen against the shadowy coast. It was a warm and welcoming sight but we were not heading there, we were heading into the night. Anton sent me down below to change into warmer clothing and in the cabin I could hear the rush of water over our hull. Dressing quickly, I pulled a pair of jeans over my shorts and slipped a nylon pack – away windcheater over my jumper. When I came out into the cockpit, Anton had changed too, he was wearing some warm-looking sailing trousers and he had reached

under the sailing horse to grab his high-collared, thick coat. He had all the equipment to enable him to stay alert and a good job too.
The cotton in my jeans seemed to absorb all the dampness in the air and I wished that I had equipped myself more suitably for the voyage. Oil-skins would have made night sailing more comfortable. I mused that this seemed far way from my experience of sailing in Greece, we never sailed beyond six o'clock in the evening. We were generally tied up at our moorings or at anchor by six thirty and showered and in the taverna by seven-thirty, sitting outside on the terrace in the warm breeze.
The off-shore wind was cool rather than cold but it was not warm and it was most moist. I shuddered with the cold and the remembrance of more pleasant times in more clement climes. As I steeped back onto the ever-darkening deck, lit only by the black oily glow of one of the hurricane lamps, I could hardly see the details of my brother's face. We swapped command, I took the tiller and he went forward, a shadowy form on the foredeck. He swayed near the bow, as he set the plumb line into the water, raised it up to the forward hurricane lamp, which cast an eerie pool of light just in front of his feet and decided how deep the channel might be.
Up ahead we noticed a cruising yacht, twenty eight foot, maybe more, a floodlit deck, and powerful lamps glowing brightly across the water in front of its bow. Ours were the smallest navigational lights that I had ever seen, theirs were like beacons, a red and green light like those found on the top of ambulances. The water all around them, it soon became clear, was floodlit like a stadium and the boat was reflected in the water by the glow as it might be in daylight.
In the case of our boat, even the bright white side of our boat was shrouded in shadows and our navigational lights, which ran of two small batteries were the size of a small indicator light, hardly visible a quarter of a nautical mile away. The cruiser on the other hand was lit up like a Christmas tree.
As we got nearer, we could hear the thud of the big diesel engines and we could see that the crew, two middle-aged couples, were drinking what we presumed was hot coffee. I have never been an envious person but that night I was visited by the green-eyed monster of jealousy. A strange spot for a picnic and rather late, I remember thinking but Anton knew what the trouble was, they had run aground.
Being Irish and living in England you have a choice, you can become more Irish than the Irish or more English than the English. My brother demonstrated our whimsical ability to become more English than the English that night. We were flying the Red Ensign, "Waterwitch" was registered in the United Kingdom so we had to obey British Maritime law; never neglect a boat in trouble. As he strolled back to get his loudhailer, a rusty, green metal cone with a stirrup handle, I heard their engines rise in pitch, rev and then there was a churning sound as the propeller was engaged. The crew of the other boat were trying to reverse off the sand bank. We were now close enough to see clearly, in their lights not ours to see what the situation was. I watched as the muddy brown water spiralled underneath their stern. The propeller and therefore the keel and rudder were stuck fast in the marsh.
"Ahoy there," Anton bellowed, "Are you in a spot of trouble.
"*Ja*, we are stuck," said the German captain.
The area was clearly a popular spot for German tourists, first the windsurfer and secondly this boat. They could have been Austrian my German dialect has never been that good.
"Oh, dear," Anton replied, pretending that he had only just spotted their predicament because he was such a polite chap. "You appear to have run aground. We'll tow you off'

Not only had Anton corrected the German by telling him he was not stuck but had run aground, he had offered to tow them off and all we had was our puny engine that hardly moved our light yacht, how could we pull a pleasure boat with all its fripperies: batteries, echo-sounder, engine, flushing loo, gas cooker, fridge, ovens, radar, radios ship-to-shore telephone, shower, and four well-fed crew.
Sailors love to use jargon, you were never stuck, you were had run aground.
The German smiled, and then noticed our boat; his smile evaporated and his mouth widened in disbelief. He recovered quickly though, there was no one else to help, he had no choice but to accept our help.
"Thank you," he said weakly.
"Throw us your stern rope and we'll have you off in a jiffy," my brother called out confidently.
It was clear the German did not know what a jiffy was; it was a nineteen thirties expression, matching our boat. They had obviously been trying to manoeuvre out of their position for some time because he shrugged the shrug of a beaten man. He must have assumed it must mean quickly because immediately afterwards he went to the stern and picked up his stern painter.
I stood by expecting the next few minutes to be interesting to watch at the very least. We were only capable of doing four knots and yet their massive diesel engines had not managed to shift their boat. I had to admire my brother for trying. The German was weak with frustration and too tired to argue.
He gathered up his rope and threw it as we passed by at a steady three knots. My brother was stationed at the mast mainstays and I had the tiller. Cool as a cucumber, Anton grabbed the mess of rope as it uncoiled, and then strode calmly along the deck to where I sat and wrapped the rope around the nearest windlass. He had straightened and untangled the rope on his passage form beam to aft and I was completely astounded by how easy he had made it look.
The rope became taught; Anton held one end and jumped into the cockpit holding on with both hands. The windlass clicked twice as it moved in a clockwise direction as he wound the rope around it. There was a creaking sound from poor old "Waterwitch", followed by a sucking sound emanating from the bow of the German boat. Her engines were still idling but it was not necessary for the diesel to become active and it may well have made things worse as the propeller shaft was clearly stuck in the mud. We came around the back of her and she swung around, off the bank and into the channel, both boats were now floating. With pride my brother unfurled the other boat's rope, jumped up onto the deck and let it slip into the water so the captain of the vessel other vessel could haul in his stern rope.
"You should be all right now," Anton said cheerfully.
"Thank you!" cried the astonished captain, his three friends joined him in a chorus of "*Danke*", accompanied by much waving. Whilst we were bathing in the light of our new found glory, saviours to stranded sailors, we hit a sandbank. It was no great thud; we just glided through the shallows and stopped. One minute I was almost glad that we were there to help and not in some warm bar with warm lights and a warm fire but in the next moment the bubble was burst.
My brother stumbled, it was a good job he had been standing with his legs apart and his arms akimbo, like Peter Pan at the time of impact, otherwise he may have landed in the water. The rate at which we hit the bank was such that he regained his balance and composure with consummate ease.

Unfortunately, the captain of the other boat noticed, the indignation, the agony and the ignominy were almost too much to bear. Before we could establish whether we were stuck fast, the German hailed us.
"Now it is us our turn to help *you*!" he cried with relish. He thought we had been condescending and this was his revenge.
Deftly, he threw the wet rope back and luckily Anton caught it and wrapped it around the windlass again. I loosened our jib, thinking that perhaps we could tack at the same time, getting onto a better beam, allowing us to really move, although I had noticed the wind had dropped yet again.
We were lucky that we had someone to get us off. The big diesels growled and the water around the propeller burbled, then we drifted easily off the bank, as gracefully as we had run aground. We were extremely grateful and enthusiastically shouted our thanks. I unkindly thought my brother might say, "You're very kind", or "Do come again, but he contented himself with "danke", "danke schon" and "thank you".
We were young, free and international. The slate was clean; we had rescued them; they had rescued us. We came about, a nautical term for turning around.
Sailing majestically towards the victims we had saved who had become our saviours, Anton decided that we could tack at the entrance of the channel that had caused both boats so much trouble, then sail along a course that would take us directly to the safety of Olhao.
I pictured the warm bar with friends we had yet to meet, a roaring fire and an ice cold drink to quench our thirst and most of all hot food. I dreamed of allowing my brother to row the tender back to "Waterwitch" and collapsing into a contented heap on my bunk falling into a lavish sleep.
It was not to be, as we approached, we noticed that the Germans had managed to get their boat lodged on the sand once again. My brother leapt into action, this time with our rope. Nevertheless, the Germans were adamant, they did not want our help, and they had decided that this game of rescuing each other from the quagmire should end. In order to prove that they did not need our help, they reversed serenely off the sandbank. In the meantime, we had narrowed our tack to offer assistance, heading to the stricken yacht. Their boat started to motor away and we hit another sand-bar. This time we hit the bank with a dull thud, such was the new speed that we had achieved on this superb tack. The Germans waved, far too enthusiastically for my liking. To this day, I am convinced that they noticed what happened and were aware that we needed their help, but they ignored us. This behaviour, I felt sure would not be tolerated in the Baltic, Barents or any other sea, or even on Boden See (Lake Constance). We called after them and their hearing which had been so acute all those minutes before seemed to have suddenly failed them. I can still see the skipper of that vessel waving and wishing us goodnight. We could hear him and he was downwind from us, how could he fail to hear us? We cursed our luck and their lack of Christian or any other form of charity. We admitted defeat, Anton secured the boat with an anchor and we both stowed the sails, all we could do was wait until the tide lifted us off the sand bank. Defeated by events and the elements, we moved inside the cabin and lit the hurricane lanterns. They spread a dim light but the sight of soft cushions and wooden walls made me feel that I was at home. A floating, moving, creaking home but dry and warm like a cave.
The talk over a warming cup of coffee, which Anton made from boiled water, heated on the primus stove, was good humoured. We had to accept our fate but we did more than once mention the ungrateful and unkind conduct of the skipper of the other yacht.

The fact that he was German never came into our assassination of his character and castigation of his behaviour; we focused on the fact that he had ignored our pleas for help and flouted all maritime and humanitarian laws. We decided that he was only a "day-sailor" and so he did not know any better. I did get my hot food, Anton cooked us a delicious supper, he was always an excellent cook. We had a hearty "one-pot-wonder". Every meal was made in one pot, a small saucepan into which my brother managed to cram wonderful ingredients and flavours.

While we settled down to scoff the rice and sauce, we realised that we were closer to Faro than we imagined; not Faro town, but Faro airport. The late night rush was on; the last flights from all over Europe were delivering passengers. Aircraft engine screamed overhead.

After supper, we came out, sat in the cockpit, covered our ears and watched as their undercarriages almost brushed our masts. The boat shuddered; we both felt the shock waves of sound reverberating around our skeletons. The sound of aircraft pierced the night. Trying to sleep in a flight path is no easy task; all we wanted was peace and yet every fifteen or twenty minutes another winged beast flew overhead roaring loudly. We waited for the one that would take off our mast.

Chapter Four

Hanging Aground, Having Run Aground

The first few planes were not so bad. They had a good height and they approached the airport high above our marshland home but the following six or seven came in low. We hurriedly cleared away our supper, still complaining that if we had not been so helpful, we would not be in this predicament, together we decided that someone of the German captain's calibre should not have been allowed loose on a boat. Conversation in a confined space where nothing happens tends to be limited and repetitive, even the simplest slight is mulled over and magnified.

A sounding after supper, to complement the one Anton had taken before hand, assured him that the tide was no longer ebbing. It was reassuring to know that we would not sink any further into the swamp. If we did, our weight would embed us in the quagmire and we might not get out. This would be disastrous because the rising tide would then flow over us rather than lift us out of the swamp. After all our hard work, it would have been a shame to see "Waterwitch" drowned in a marsh. It was decided that we would have to wait four hours for high tide and that sleep was the best course of action.

My complaint that it might be difficult to sleep within a stone's throw of one of Europe's busiest airports met with a broad smile.

"I can offer you a copy of Erskine Childers's book, *"The Riddle of the Sands*" if you like."

"Thank you, I've heard of it," I replied, always willing to better myself.

"It's set in the Baltic and the protagonists are always running aground."

"I know where the Baltic is and if I wanted a holiday like that, I would have gone to the Fenland marshes.

"I suppose you regret reading *"Swallows and Amazons"* in the first place."

"I read it; I didn't want to live it."

"I thought the book got you interested in sailing in the first place."

"I'll admit the book did glamorise sailing and stimulated my involvement with wind and water, I should have left it to the professionals."

“Thanks very much.”
“Oh, I didn’t mean it like that; I’m just a bit cold and shell shocked from the bombardment of aircraft noise.”
As if to illustrate my point another one came over drowning out any chance for conversation.
“It is a bit noisy.”
“Never mind, I have a full belly, a steaming cup of coffee, dry, warm blankets and a shelter of sorts, life *is* not so bad after all.”
“That’s the attitude to have!”
“At least we’re out of the harbour.”
“We’re still afloat, just.”
“Do you think we’ll make Olhao tomorrow?”
“We’ll be there for lunch, no problem.”
“I hope so.”
“We’ve just had a bad day.”
“It can only get better, right?”
“Of course, I reckon that it will take about four hours to reach the island.”
“Who’s going to do the first watch?”
“No one, we’re in a shallow channel, we’re at anchor as well as being aground, no one would come down here in the day, let alone at night with the tide out. Our German friend was just lost and had not reckoned on the tide variations being so marked. We’re quite safe.”
A plane roared overhead, looking like it was going to clip the mast. Our dim navigational lights would be invisible from the air, I assumed.
“Good, we just need the flights to stop; surely this airport is not twenty four hours.”
“It’s not, they’ll stop soon. We’ll both get some rest and move out early in the morning.”
“I’m off to bed.”
“See you in the morning. I was hoping we might drift off with the current but that’s not happening. I’ll check the anchor’s secure and set the alarm for high tide. We should be able to get off, then.”
“How will you know when high tide is?”
“I got that information from the harbour office.”
“Fine, sleep well.”
“I will. You too.”
In the cabin, I slipped off my jeans and shorts, peeled off my jumper and t-shirt and slipped naked into the cold cotton of the lined sleeping bag. At the foot of the bed were two folded acrylic rugs. Sitting up, I tossed my clothes on to the bunk opposite and draped the two synthetic blankets over my legs, then unfolded them up to my chest. I curled into a foetal position, unconcerned at not having brushed my teeth. I made a contract with myself that I would brush them doubly well the next day. We had managed to shower twice a day in Vilamoura harbour so I felt one day without washing would do no harm, we were camping after all. I was content to think about the shower I would have when we reached the island off Olhao.
By now, I was sued to the dampness in the cabin, even in harbour the whole boat would fill with dew. I would air my old clothes on deck railings the next day and change into something packed in the dry sailing bag, I had stowed at the back of the cabin. After over two weeks away, I still had clean underwear, but I worried about how I would wash our clothes now that I was down to my last clean t-shirt, my last pair of clean trousers and my last two pairs of underpants.

My head lay on the pillow and my eyes closed, I could feel my head spinning with exhaustion and I could hear the water lapping against our wooden hull. I was safe and secure and asleep almost immediately.
It was morning somewhere in the world when we woke up, but it was still night in Portugal. The airport was in silence and the lights of Faro seemed to glow more brightly in the clear night.
I slipped on my beige shorts and jumper and barefoot, I joined Anton on deck.
"How long have you been up?"
"Not long, I'm glad you're awake you can help me."
"I heard you moving about."
"Did I wake you?"
"I don't think so, is everything all right?"
"I think so; the water is coming into the channel faster than I thought."
"So we need to move the boat."
"If we can."
Anton dropped down into the cave and extracted two boats hooks and armed with one each, we moved towards the bow of the boat. Standing either side of the prow, we sank the long rods into the water.
"Right," said my brother." Just push your boat hook into the marsh and we'll punt this thing off."
The anchor chain was loosed, we were being held in place purely by the mud. My boathook squelched into the mud and water splashed as I raised it again. I looked at Anton and he looked at me.
"Together, one, two, three!" he cried.
Holding our palms over the top and leaning heavily on our arms, we pushed our lances into the bank and heaved. A sigh came from the bow and "Waterwitch" started to drift off, we were free. My brother laid down his boathook and hauled up the anchor as we drifted backwards off the underground mound. I was told to go to the stern and take the tiller.
I left my boathook on the beam and hurried back to the cockpit where I unleashed the rope that tied the tiller, pulling hard to port and the boat swung around drifting on the eddy currents. We moved down the channel and I straightened her up. Silently, like commandos, we eased our way along the widening stretch of water to the mouth of the channel, the current propelling us.
Anton took soundings and when the depth reached fourteen feet, he turned of the torch and picked up the anchor. Tossing it over the side, the splash pierced the night and some marsh birds squealed at the disturbance, their panic echoing in the silence. Using the navigation lights, he moved back to the cockpit carrying both boathooks. He stowed them and then sat on the bench beside me.
"Right, back to bed, I'll do the rest. I'll put the sea-anchor out, at the stern, and that will stop us spinning during the night."
The sea anchor was basically a canvas bag on a rope; unbelievably it did a wonderful job, just filling with water. I assumed that rocks could be added to the bag to give greater stability. Nothing could beat a chain anchor fastened to the sea bed but the sea-anchor came close.
"The alarm is set for the next high tide, I don't feel able to take her through in this darkness."
A nod from me showed that I concurred with his view. I slipped into the cabin, slipped off my clothes and slipped into my warm bed. It had been cold out on the deck and even after only ten minutes, in the cold night air, despite my cotton jumper, I

longed to be back in my cocoon, asleep. Hardly had I curled up and dozed off than I was awakened. Six hours had elapsed and yet I still felt as if I was suffering from severe fatigue. The sea air had left me exhausted; yet I was under twenty, fit and lean. I obviously lacked stamina. In truth we had been burning the candles at both ends, staying up late and getting up early. The two parties that I had been to before we left had not helped.

Out on deck it was sunny but not warm, a cold breeze made the stanchions crack, the shrouds jingled in their housings, the ensign fluttered; all formed our on board wind vane. I wiped my eyes and scratched my chin; the bristles itched. I was growing a beard, shaving in harbour is fine, but out to sea, I decided I would not bother. Indeed shaving at sea could be fatal, I did not fancy having shaving scars all over my face. My brother was sporting a blond beard and within a few weeks, I would have one too, I could shave in Ibiza.

Taking a quick wash, splashing a small amount of water into a plastic bowl filled from the jerry can, I wondered when I would be able to have my next proper bath. The showers at the harbour had been adequate and the pipes had flowed with hot water. From now on there was only going to be cold fresh water or the sea. We had two bars of soap, coal tar for the fresh water and sea-soap for the briny; it was especially formulated to lather in seawater.

Looking over the side of the boat and feeling the cold wind on my arms, I decided to stop at just cleaning my face. My towel was damp and musty smelling, as was all the gear, in the boat, every morning. That was why I despised camping, getting into soggy clothes. As a child I had been spoilt, warm folded clothes had come straight for the airing cupboard, which always made me feel cosy.

Anton had put the kettle on the boil so I made us some coffee, rinsing out the dirty mugs with hot water form the kettle before adding instant coffee and dried milk and allowing the water to boil properly. Sugar was a luxury so we did without.

Sipping our beverages, we sat next to each other on the wooden plank that we called the sailing-horse and which served as a cockpit seat. The tiller stood between us and I rested a foot on the wooden arm. I let the other leg dangle, hugged my cup of coffee and looked out over the marsh for the first time. The airport was well camouflaged; Faro was practically invisible now the landing lights were not silhouetted against the night sky. It lay beside the rising sun, a blurred outline on the horizon.

I had not combed my hair and I felt it ruffled pleasantly by the gentle wind. Sipping the hot fluid, which warmed my insides, I looked around for any sign of life. If we were in a wildlife haven, they were keeping a low profile. I craned my head both left and right and saw nothing but flats and water. We were totally alone. Our road map would not show us where we were. We had stumbled on this enclave but we did not want to be here and we were not sure of how to get out of the maze of channels. Hunger kept us from worrying too much about our predicament.

We decided to eat before moving pulling off. The bread was soft still and the apricot jam was delicious. The food was good, the location peaceful and calming, the sun was beginning to climb, warming us, and even the wind seemed less chilled with two cups of hot liquid in our bellies.

The impression given might be of a foolhardy adventure, our voyage an eccentric and doomed undertaking. This was not the case. My brother was and is a fine navigator; he had a good compass, sextant and all the other necessary hand-held navigational instruments. Like sailors in the thirties, we had all the basics; we only lacked a wireless transmitter, radar and sonar.

Anton could judge our speed and the distance that we travelled extremely accurately and he could plot a course as well as anyone, his navigational and sailing skills were second to none. Any sailing depends on different factors; that is why it is considered a dangerous and thrilling sport, even if the only danger is capsizing in a dinghy in shallow, safe waters. Tide and time wait for no man, currents change; winds whip themselves into a frenzy or gently stroke your face. Variables affect any voyage.
Our first outing in "Waterwitch" had been most unfortunate. The wind was not playing our game; she blew gently from the wrong direction, when we wanted her to push us along. A force five on the "Beaufort Scale" would have suited us perfectly. The coastline was unforgiving; there was no separate sand and sea here, more a mixture of the two. The clay soil absorbing the water that it should be resisting and coupled to this the sea deposited its load of sand against the sodden soil, forming sandbanks.
We were equipped for the ocean, sailing in open seas, the boat and its crew did not stand a chance in this bog. A narrow boat with its shallow hull was more suited to these channels. It was, however, too late to exchange our vessel. She was in unfamiliar waters, a foreigner in a strange land; we needed to take her home, back to the ocean waves, where her free spirit, long mast and deep keel should be given free rein.
We set off hopefully "Waterwitch" and my brother straining to get free of the shallows. I had been imbued with an unhealthy cynicism, which I kept form my brother for fear of upsetting him. We had wanted to go from A to B and now we were at C; there was nothing I could do. I had been too impatient to get to sea and too willing to head for B. I was in their hands, the elements, the boat and my brother. I would have to row along with them and sail side by side with them.
So there I stood, in my damp clothes, watching the murky water for any sign of a sandbank, my boat hook in one hand, ready to fend off any outcrops that we came close towards.
There was little use in taking soundings; we had to follow the channel. If our keel struck an outcrop or mound under the water, we would have to deal with that if and hewn it happened. My job was to fend off any land-masses on our port beam. I would literally push the boat way from it.
The starboard side was clear and we raced on, ever vigilant and primed in case there was any sudden contact with land.
We still had an hour before the tide started to turn. When the tide went out, we would have to close haul the sails and punt our way through the shallows. We both hoped this would not be the case; "Waterwitch" had been knocked around enough over the last sixteen hours. She had rescued a fellow damsel in distress and been abandoned by her younger and stronger sister, left to wallow in the shallows and miseries of her outrageous fortune.

Chapter Five

The Sea, the Open Sea, the Ever Free

Soon we were free from the swamp and out into the open sea but by that time it was eleven o'clock already. We held our course south, south-east for an hour, before tacking and heading east into the true entrance to the channel at Olhao. We clipped along merrily and within three hours we could see the navigation lights of the port, red and green that demarcated the entrance to the harbour. They were lit even in the dusk

We had eaten lunch on the move during our three-hour tack. Anton had been sailing and I was the galley boy. I made some salami sandwiches with the last of the bread, some slices of cheese added. We were allowed to use the last of our fresh provisions because we were nearing our destination so I used a quarter of the remaining stick of bread for each sandwich, the bread was hardening nicely so it was a chewy and satisfying snack.

There was still some hard cheese left and we had enough tinned food to keep us going for three weeks. Anton ate his sandwich at the helm and I ate mine sitting on the windward side, spray splashing my face. I had bought out two small bottles of beer and we clamped the bottles between our knees as "Waterwitch" lurched determinedly through the rising breakers. This was sailing. It was a little overcast, but it was fairly warm. The wind was not icy but cold nonetheless so we wore our anoraks.

We had not quite reached Olhao by lunchtime as we had planned but this was due to the direction of the wind and the course we were forced by the elements to take. Our eldest brother, Patrick, was due to join us in Gibraltar in six days time, there was no pressure, I thought, having no idea how long it would take us to get along the coast of Spain. The wind continued to daunt us. We made swift progress on one tack and then scant progress on the next.

Eventually, at three o'clock, according to the yacht's clock, we prepared for our final approach to the harbour. It would entail sailing up a wide channel to the northwest of the town and then turning about and heading for the harbour, passing the entrance on the same tack, heading for the island, perhaps making several small tacks on our journey there. In handwriting terms we were making the first two strokes of a capital 'N' starting at the base on the left.

All we could see was the harbour wall and it was to the left of that we were headed. Once we passed the western wall of the port, we would set another course. I took the helm, Anton went below to work out measurements and write the log. The salt air had made my lips dry, so I licked them, enjoying the saline flavour. My arms felt more burnt than brown, another reason for wearing my anorak. I had rolled up the sleeves to my elbow and my forearms stung, they had not felt this sore in the marina but I noticed a dusting of dry salt on them. The wind was cold enough to make the blond hairs stand on end. It was bizarre, my arms were hot, but I still had goose pimples, salted goose bumps.

Anton came back up on deck and looked around us, checked the log and went forward to the bow. When he came back to the cockpit, he sat beside me.

"Now, you see that buoy on the port side, the red one at eleven o'clock? Set a course for that," he said. "We're doing five knots and our compass bearing is 355 degrees, so just keep the compass needle on that heading."

Ever dutiful and wanting to be a useful member of the crew, I steered for the boy, moving the tiller handle so that the bow of "Waterwitch" was aiming straight at it. I held the tiller, which swayed slightly in the movement of the waves. Anton decided that we could use a more efficient jib, a racing one, for our dash past the harbour and so he went below to rummage around. In a few minutes, I saw the hatch on the fore-deck above his cabin, open up.
I looked down at the compass and noticed we were heading at 345 degrees, I a full ten degrees of course, I looked up at the buoy and it still seemed to be at eleven o'clock but perhaps the offshore current was pushing us of course, I moved the tiller arm until we were at 356 degrees to compensate. The buoy started to move along the port bow and disappear behind the sheets, so I gently pushed the tiller away from me. We hit several high waves in succession and the compass now read 343 and the buoy had disappeared behind the bow. I pulled the tiller towards me and we started to head along at 355 again. It was hard work, constantly readjusting the sensitive tiller, keeping an eye on the compass, the buoy and the sheets, making sure the sails were filled and not flapping. For ten minutes, I kept her on course. My brother's head poked up from through the hatch again.
"Are we at the buoy yet?" he asked.
"Getting nearer," I replied.
Anton obviously wanted to change sails just before or after we tacked. It had seemed that we were getting nearer but in fact we were not. I couldn't believe it took so long. Perhaps our speed was not correct. It showed three knots, the wind had dropped noticeably or had I just got used to the howling and flapping in my ears? My brother fed the bright, red, racing jib through the hold and onto the deck. He followed the sail, climbing through the forward hatch and stood on the deck, looking around. I knew what his next question would be and I hated to give him the answer, we were no closer to the buoy. He moved skilfully over the boat and jumped down into the cockpit next to me.
"Oh for goodness sake," he complained. "Can't you do the simplest thing? All I asked you to do was to steer for that buoy."
We were both tired from our long days and particularly from our lack of sleep while stuck in the marsh.
"But I am steering for the buoy, our course is still 355," I argued, feeling that it was my fault.
"Then why aren't we there?"
"I don't know."
"I should have done it myself."
"You can't do all the work."
"I know."
"Sorry."
I need a drink to warm me up, do you want a tot?
"No, thanks."
He scuttled downstairs into the cabin and came back up carrying a shot glass and a bottle of the local firewater, stopped with a cork. He bit into the stopper and wrenched it from the bottle with his teeth, spat the cork at his feet and shivered. He was very cold. Taking the bottle in one hand, dispensing with the glass, he took a large swig and swallowed.
"Oh, damn," he cried, slamming the bottle down on the roof of the cabin and wiping his mouth. "That's the paraffin."

I felt so sorry for his mistake that I could not laugh; he had swallowed a whole mouthful of lamp fuel instead of the local spirit.
"Are you okay? I asked. "Drink some water."
"Water? I need something stronger than that to get the taste out of my mouth. Where's the special brandy?"
"Where you left it last night, I think."
He found the bottle in the cave under the tiller, reached out and took the bottle, unscrewed the cap and took two thirsty draughts, the second of which he swilled around his mouth and gargled.
"Give me the tiller," he said in a soft, resigned voice.
I jumped up and made way for him.
"I'll stow the bottle," I said, taking the bottle from his hand and slipping it back into its place in the cave.
"I can't understand it," he said eventually, he was calm.
"Nor can I, the buoys aren't moving."
"No but we can be. What if the tide is coming out at three knots and we're travelling at the same speed? That would account for it."
"I hadn't thought of the tide at all. My experience has only been in Portsmouth Sound in dinghies, it's so deep that we didn't notice the tide. In Greece, the tide range is only a matter of inches."
"Well, that must be the answer. We've a fairly strong wind in our favour."
"So as I've been sailing towards the buoy at three knots, the tide has been flowing out at the same speed, we've been standing still, treading water. What can we do about it?"
"With luck, we've made enough progress; we should make it through the harbour channel and into the bay on one tack. We have to try, we have no choice."
"I'm up for it, but just on one condition."
"What's that?"
"You don't have another drink until we reach land."
"We'll be too busy for that. Help me with the racing jib and then we'll both put on some warmer clothes."
He lashed the tiller to the sailing horse and slackened the foresail sheets. I went forward and pulled down the jib undoing the halyards. The foresail slid down the cable. I allowed the jib to fall slowly and as each section passed me, I unhooked the hanks and furled the sail. As quickly as this happened, Anton was clipping on the racing jib. He clipped the bottom end or foot to the forestay, on the prow, then gave me the signal to hoist. As I pulled on the halyard and wound the winch, he was fixing each hank onto the halyard.
The jib billowed with wind as I raised it. Anton was already back at the tiller by the time the sail was fully hoisted. The mainsail had kept us steady and we really started to move once Anton was at the helm and the new sail filled with wind. We healed over as I folded, bagged and stowed the old jib, throwing the bag through the hatch and on to the bunk in the forward cabin. I closed the hatch and hung on to the mast, feeling the spray splashing up on my feet and thighs as "Waterwitch" cleaved a path through the water.

Chapter Six

Olhao Ahoy!

It was late afternoon on a cool day and I stood at the prow of the boat. I had dressed more warmly and my jeans that I had intended to wear occasionally had become a dirty uniform. I wore a dry sweater, crew neck of course, and my trusty anorak. Despite the cold, I felt warmed by the exhilaration and hope as this proud vessel did what it did best and was designed to do, race.

"Ready about," Anton cried.

I trotted unsteadily to my position beside him, almost slipping on the sloping deck.

"Jive, ho," he called, satisfied I was ready.

Releasing the sheets as he pushed the tiller away from him, the boat came about in a wide arc. The main sheet was released as we commenced our turn and all the sails flapped wildly. The boom swung around as we started to point in the opposite direction. I pulled hard on the jib sheet and the sail came around onto my side of the boat. The wind ballooned the nylon and satisfied with the course and fullness of both sails, Anton told me to pull in the foresail a fraction more. The windlass drum clicked twice and I forced a part of the remaining rope into the clam jam cleat, which was just in front of and below the windlass.

My brother held the tiller as he instructed me on how to effectively trim the main sail. The wind was howling in our ears and the spray from both sides of the boat splashed into the cockpit space. We were moving now and the harbour was getting closer. Nothing could stop us now. Olhao was a fishing port, commercial through and through. The early morning fishing boats had tied up long ago and the evening fleet would have a few hours of work to go. We could see no ships taking the catch to canneries and we were certain that no small boats would be in the area until nightfall drove them back to safety. The drifters were slow lumbering craft and we felt sure that we could outrun them. Besides, the tide was ebbing fast and most ships would stay out until it flowed again. My brother was pleased and I was relieved. We had an uninterrupted line to our target.

"We're doing nine knots, this is terrific," Anton said. "I'll slow down to about six knots when we get near the harbour. You'd better get forward and keep a look out for any banks that might be ahead. Get the anchor ready to drop, we'll anchor one we're passed the port. The island isn't far away. We'll either have enough speed to sail there or we'll anchor and row there in the tender, it all depends on what the draught is like on the other side."

"Aye, Aye, skipper," I replied, I was enjoying myself.

I grabbed my thick jacket from inside the cabin and put it over my light anorak, slipping into it as I made my way form the cabin and cockpit to the bow.

I was concerned about the ebbing tide bringing the keel closer to the sea bed but that would not be a worry until we got to the other side of Olhao. I was focused on getting to our goal.

Feeling elated by our progress, I watched the water rushing by, foam topped waves lapping against the spruce hull. The sails formed a shadow of the sitka spruce deck. It was a wonderful sight. I moved forward to take up position by the anchor. It was almost twilight, but we reckoned darkness was at least an hour away. The dimming light and the cloudy sky made me feel colder. I was not worried, even if those grey clouds warned of a storm, we would shortly be in the bar eating hot food served on a proper china plate with chips and salad on the side.

"Waterwitch" cut through the waves rearing slightly at each crest. The waves were rising higher as the wind picked up more. I waited to be told that we had achieved ten knots. We had to ease off from the wind to clear the harbour as we approached the wall but we might just make double-digit speed before hand. The current was flowing out, but still we didn't want to get too close to the rocks protecting the harbour wall, especially as there might be areas of eddies.

A sandbank lay directly opposite the harbour wall and a dredging ship was anchored there, its crane scooping up the sand and mud from the sea-bed and depositing it via a conveyor belt into the hold. The harbour needed to be dredged daily to keep the fishing boat channel open. This had not always been the case. The town had been a fishing port for many centuries but now that the new harbour wall with its rocks stacked against it to stop erosion jutted out into the channel, the narrowing of the passage had resulted in more deposits being dropped, making for a tight channel. Larger fishing vessels and ships to take the fish to other markets or tinning facilities had also changed the profile of the land and sea.

We had a choice of either a "pell-mell" dash through the channel, with the danger of hitting the harbour wall or the dredger or alternatively easing off our course and sailing majestically through at five or six knots. After our earlier experience, we erred on the side of caution. I stood at the bow railings, looking over the side as we came through the channel. On either side of us was a sandbank invisible at high tide but now ominously present. Each minute more of the sand was visible. The water was draining from the area and draining rapidly.

We had about ten feet either side, so there was little danger of us hitting the banks. Having no idea how far the island was and how deep the water that led to it would be, Anton, seeing our situation, instructed me to put down the boathook and pick up the anchor. I stood pressed against the bow railing, my feet apart, looking almost like a figurehead from an old "Man of War". The railings reached a few inches below my knee and my shins rested against the supports. I looked forward to the day when I could sit on the bow holding onto the railings as we raced at ten knots on a sunny, hot day.

Instead, I was contented to with the wisps of spray that soaked my trousers and slipped off the nylon of my ski-ing jacket. It was waterproof and warm; I was pleased that I had worn it on our trip out to the airport because it had been so cold in London. I did not mind my jeans getting soaked. As long as my torso was in a cocoon, the extremities could be a little damp.

However cold it was out here in Portugal, it could not compete with the cold front that had come to England in May, making it feel as though the country was still in February. For the first time since we had left Vilmaoura, I felt happy. This was what I had come to do, sail through the elements to a safe haven. I could picture the warmth of the bar in my mind's eye. As we sped along the channel, I wondered at our swift progress, we were really moving fast. This was a side of sailing that I had not as yet seen on this trip. So far we had drifted quietly along, now we were motoring. It was a glorious strong wind in our sails. Five knots does not sound fast, nor does ten, but when you are up at the prow of a boat as it cuts through the water, slicing waves in its path, canvas alone pushing you on, you feel as if you are flying.

The racing jib with its brash colour and nylon skin contrasted with our original, grubby, beige, canvas mainsail but its fullness drove us on even more efficiently. The canvas mainsail was taut with wind too and straining. The aluminium mast, that had replaced the original wooden one, was creaking in its wooden housing. Ahead of the mast the jib, a perfect triangle, did not flap a bit. It was at full stretch and hauled in tight. The sights, sounds and smells aboard a yacht, nothing could beat them and the feeling of freedom. The sight of water passing underneath and the port revealing more of itself as we got nearer, the broad bow of the dredger becoming clearer all the time, I was on cloud nine.

Then it happened. There was thud, like a distant drumbeat, and we stopped dead in the water. I was caught off guard and lost my balance, the heavy anchor adding to my inability to regain control. How I managed not to end up in the drink, as sailors call the sea, I shall never know. I had hit both shins against hard metal; I swayed back and forth, the anchor dragging me to and fro as it swung like a weight on a pendulum. By the fifth sway, I had steadied myself and I slipped the anchor on to the deck, letting the chain slip through my fingers as the anchor came to a rest on its side. Perhaps it was because my legs were braced against the prow and slightly bent that the shock was absorbed, like ski-ing on moguls. Both legs felt bruised from the hard contacted sustained by the railings. It was the least fleshy part of my legs and I winced.

"Are you okay?" Anton asked, calling from the stern.

"Fine," I stammered, I was still upright after all. "What happened?"

"It looks like the keel has hit a sand bank, the tide's pretty low."

"What do we do now?"

"Over the side, we'll have to take down the sails and secure the boat before we topple over."

I had the jib down in record time, furled but not stowed. My brother dealt with the mainsail. As I slipped off my jeans and took off my shoes, he tied the canvas around the boom. I striped out of my top layer and he too slipped out of his oilskins and clothes. We tossed them through the forward hatch with the jib. He was wearing swimming shorts underneath; we peeled off our t-shirts together and threw them in the hold. It was cold but we were not worried about that, nor were we worried about the ridiculous sight we must have made.

"Right, we go over the side, each with one of these." He was holding two strands of thin steel cable, the halyard that went up to the top of the mast. "The first thing we do is secure the boat by the mast. Untie your anchor at the bow; I'll untie the anchor at stern. Attach it to the end of your cable and that should hold her. I don't know how deep the keel is in, but we need to spread the weight. The mast is aluminium and it we can keep her upright it should keep the pressure off the keel."

We went to work and the two metal wires from the top of the mast were connected to the anchors. Our mast would be like the tier of a suspension bridge. The tension would stop the boat from lurching and snapping off the keel. We would have to secure the anchors well if we did not want a broken boat.

"Okay, once in the water, swim out as far as you can and plant the anchor deep. We can winch in any slack from on board. We'll wedge some planks of wood and the boathooks against the hull later."

I jumped into water, without the anchor, Anton would pass it down to me. I bent my knees ready to bomb, there was small splash and I stood up, I had it the bottom. The water was below my knees and it seemed to be trickling away like water out of a bath when the plug is pulled. To see the tide ebbing at such an alarming rate was a very

worrying sight. Every second more of the sea bed was revealed. It is best observed from a distance not in the thick of it.
"Don't swim run!" Anton called out smiling. He handed me down the anchor. I pictured him lowering down his anchored and then slipping over the side, jumping into the shallows. Neither of us would have contemplated jumping into the water with anything in our hands, tempting as it might have been in our panic.
"I thought it might be deeper!" I shouted back as I scurried over the beach, through puddles and across compacted sand. Soon the wire became taut so I planted the anchor securely and ran back to the boat.
My brother, dynamo that he was, was already at work wedging wood under the hull; I hoped he had spent as much time digging in his anchor as I had mine, but the taut wire above our heads confirmed that the boat was suspended at ninety degrees vertically. It was now like a suspension bridge, the weight shared by the cables.
We could not see the keel, nor did we want to. The water was now only a half meter deep, about a foot and half, and we no way of knowing how far it would fall. A boat hook was wedged on either side in the sand under the hull, in the middle, across the beam. Two thick planks were similarly supporting the aft and bow. Anton pulled himself up aboard the boat and I went around to the other side. Handing down two more planks and the other boathook, he smiled.
"We're in deep water, now," he noted dryly.
"Up the channel without a paddle," I replied.
"That's an idea. We'll sue the spare oars from the dinghy as well. Luckily we have tow pairs, just in case."
He smiled at me again and I smiled back although I did not feel like it. I secured the starboard side, quite happy to be out of the boat. The paddles were handed down and I was directed as to where to put them, a metre away from the boathooks.
"You can come up now," he called.
I would rather have stayed where I was but it was lonely on the mud flats and it was a long walk to Olhao. I heaved myself up off our little beach and into the cockpit. The wood had a hollow echo to it as I walked over to the cabin to look inside. There were no cracks in the hull that I could see. My brother was still tightening the steel cables that held the anchors, perhaps we would not fall over after all.
"Okay," he explained. "This is the story. The keel is five foot, more or less, and we cannot see how much is stuck in the sand bank. As the water is about a foot deep now, we can assume that four foot of keel is embedded."
"The water is about a foot now; that makes three foot eleven in the sand."
"Quite the mathematician."
Thank you."
"So, we have little choice. There are two possibilities. The water will drain away completely and the boat might keel over, so we can't leave her alone, we'll have to have someone on board to send up a flare. The other scenario is that the tide will come in and the keel is stuck fast, therefore we will sink as the water rises and the boat does not.
"In that case, I'll walk to the island and you stay with the boat."
"It's a bit more difficult than that."

TIMELINE FROM: http://www.fsmitha.com/time/1982.html

Jan 1 Another military coup in Ghana. Exuberant soldiers loot homes and shops.

Jan 7 Ghana's new military regime, led by Jerry Rawlings, announces the creation of tribunals for "revolutionary justice" regarding "crimes against the people."

Jan 12 The Rawlings regime announces the return of diplomatic relations between Ghana and Libya. Libya's leader, Gaddafi, has sent a message of solidarity with Ghana's "revolution."

Jan 26 Unemployment in Britain increases by 129,918 to 3,070,621 - a post-war record.

Feb 2 In Hama, a Syrian city of 350,000, Muslim Brotherhood insurgents have taken power, driving out Baathist authorities and declaring the city liberated. With tanks and air power, Syria's Baathist president, Hafez al Assad, crushes the Brotherhood.

Feb 25 The European Court of Human Rights rules that teachers who beat children against the wishes of the parents are in breach of the Human Rights Convention.

Mar 10 The United States describes Libya as supporting terrorism and subversion and places an embargo on Libyan oil imports.

Mar 13 Colonel Gaddafi describes President Reagan as a "destructive person" and a "terrorist."

Mar 22 In Nicaragua the Sandinista government has been criticized for forcibly removing some 10,000 Miskito Indians from land along the Honduran border.

Apr 2 The military junta in Argentina lands troops in British-ruled Falkland Islands, which Argentines call the Malvinas and consider Argentinean.

Apr 3 Prime Minister Thatcher announces the despatch of a naval task force to the Falklands.

Apr 5 Britain's government in Falklands surrenders.

Apr 25 Israel completes its withdrawal from the Sinai Peninsula in keeping with the Israel-Egypt Peace Treaty of 1979.

May 2 A British nuclear submarine sinks an Argentine Navy cruiser, killing 323 sailors.

May 4 An Argentine missile hits a British light cruiser, killing 20.

May 8 Anton and I arrive in Portugal.

May 20 Waterwitch sets sail.

May 24 Iranian troops retake the border town of Khorramshahr, 40 kilometres southeast of Basra, capturing 19,000 Iraqi soldiers. They execute 2,000 of their prisoners in retaliation for the rape of Iranian women at the beginning of the war.

May 29 British paratroopers defeat a larger force of Argentine troops in the first land battle of the Falklands.

May 30 Spain becomes the 16th member of NATO.

Jun 3 In London, Israel's ambassador to Britain is shot and critically wounded by the Palestinian terrorist organization led by Abu Nidal.

Jun 4 Palestinians have been launching attacks against Israelis from southern Lebanon, including rocket and artillery attacks across the border into northern Israel. Israel bombs a Palestine Liberation Organization (PLO) ammunition depots and training bases. The PLO retaliates by shelling Israeli settlements.

Jun 6 Israel invades southern Lebanon, an operation the Israelis call "'Operation Peace for Galilee."

Jun 9 Israeli forces have engaged Syrian forces and forced them to withdraw to Lebanon's Bekaa Valley. Israeli troops are on the perimeter of the city of Beirut. They send airplanes against trapped PLO there, and they begin patrolling all roads in and out of the city.

Jun 11 The Sandinista regime says that they have killed 21 "counterrevolutionaries" in recent days near the Honduran border. Those fighting the Sandinista regime from Honduras have been described as former National Guard soldiers who fled Nicaragua when the Sandinistas overthrew the Somoza regime.

Jun 13 Inflation has dropped to 7 percent, but the nation is in a recession and unemployment is rising. President Reagan's budget director, David A. Stockman, tells the U. S. Chamber of Commerce that the nation should stick with President Reagan's policies.

Jun 14 In the Falklands, at Stanley, the commander of Argentina's forces, General Mario Menéndez, surrenders to British Major General Jeremy Moore.

Jun 15-16 In Argentina, policemen disperse crowds angered by the surrender to the British.

Jun 16 Returning to her residence at 10 Downing Street, Prime Minister Margaret Thatcher is cheered by a crowed behind police barricades. They sing "Rule, Britannia"

Jun 18 In Argentina, junta leader General Leopoldo Galtieri, who started the Falklands War, resigns.

Jun 18 In the U.S., the Census Bureau reports that the number of families headed by one parent had doubled since 1970, caused primarily by divorce.

Jun 19 Total dead in the Falklands War: 649 for Argentina, 258 for Britain.

Jun 21 The Princess of Wales, Diana, gives birth to her first son, William.

Jun 25 Governor Rex Hunt returns to his position as Commissioner of the Falklands.

Jul 14 My mother's birthday, Bastille Day in France.

Jul 20 The Provisional IRA detonates 2 bombs in central London, killing 8 soldiers, wounding 47 others and killing 7 horses.

So while we sailed, Ghana suffered, British soldiers died abroad and at home, families from Argentina, England, The Falklands, Ireland and Ghana lost their loved ones. The IRA killed Irish troops or policemen as well as English people. Ghana and Ireland and the Falklands and England saw people hoping for basic human rights, safety to go about their lives; I wonder how much the world has changed. I changed on my trip on "Waterwitch", I think my brother did and perhaps we changed the lives of the people we met in a positive way, I hope so, after all as governments fight and fuss all we can do is respect each person who puts bread on the table and who cares for their family. I take my hat off to them and to the hardy fishermen of the Iberian Peninsular, the cargo ship crews and the oil rig workers, to all men and women who make their living from the see, in canneries and in factories or in boats and ships and to those on the land who provide us with the food and the tools to take on the most frightening and unpredictable of foes, our friend the sea.

BASIC SAILING: Sailing Terms

A	
abeam	Directly to the side of the boat.
about	On the opposite tack.
aft	At or near the stern.
aloft	Above the deck.
astern	Behind the boat.
B	
backstay	Any single wire supporting the mast from the stern.
batten	Thin wooden strips fitted into pockets for stiffening the leech of a sail.
beam	Measurement of the width of a boat.
beam reach	Sailing with the wind coming across the boat's beam.
beam wind	A wind at right angles to a boat's course.
beat	Sailing against the wind by tacking (sailing a zigzag course towards the wind).
beating to windward	To sail to windward close-hauled, tacking as you go, to reach an objective to windward.
bend	To connect two ropes with a knot.

block	A pulley.
bollard	A short heavy post on a pier or boat used for fastening docking lines.
boom	Spar that takes the foot of a sail.
bow	The forward part of a boat.
buoy	Floating navigational marker.
C	
chain plate	Metal fitting bolted to the side of a boat to hold the ends of stays and shrouds.
cleat	Fitting to which a line is secured, without knotting.
clew	Aft bottom corner of a sail, where the foot and leech meet.
come about	To change course so as to be sailing at the same angle but with the wind on the other side.
course	The direction in which a vessel is steered, usually given in degrees.
D	
dinghy	A small boat used to ferry people to a yacht; also used for sailing or rowing; also called a tender.
F	
foot	A sail's lower edge.
fore	At or toward the boat's bow.

fore-and-aft	Lengthwise, in the direction of the keel.
foremast	Mast nearest to the bow.
forestay	The foremost stay, running from the masthead to the bow.
furl	Tightly roll up a sail.
G	
gaff	Spar that secures the head of a fore-and-aft sail.
galley	A kitchen on a boat.
Genoa	Large headsail, which overlaps the mainsail.
grommet	Rope or brass ring in a sail or piece of canvas.
gunwales	Upper edges of a boat's sides.
guy	Adjustable steadying rope of a boat's rig.
H	
halyard	Line used for hoisting sails.
hank	Fitting used to attach the luff of a sail to a stay.
head	A sail's top corner; also a boat's toilet.
headsail	Sail forward of the foremast.
head stay	A forward stay.
headway	Moving forward.

heel	A boat's angle to horizontal, to lean over to one side.
helm	Tiller or wheel.
hoist	The length of the luff of a fore-and-aft sail.
hull	The body of boat.
J	
jib	A triangular headsail set on a stay forward of the foremast.
jibing	Changing direction with the wind aft; to change from one tack to another by turning the stern through the wind; also spelled gibing.
jib sheet	Line that controls the jib.
K	
keel	Centre-line backbone at the bottom of a boat.
L	
lashing	A rope used for securing any movable object in place.
lee	The side opposite that from which the wind blows; the opposite of weather.
leech	Outside edge of a sail.
lee helm	The tendency of a boat to swing leeward unless held on course.
leeward	Away from the wind; the direction to which the wind

	blows, down wind.
line	Any length of rope that has a specified use.
luff	To get so close to the wind that the sail flaps; also the forward edge of a sail.
M	
mainmast	Principal mast on a boat.
mainsail	boomed sail projecting aft from the mainmast
mainsheet	Line that controls the main boom.
make fast	Secure a line.
mast	Vertical spar to which the sails and rigging are attached.
masthead	Top of the mast.
mizzen	The shorter, after-mast on a ketch or yawl.
P	
painter	The bow line by which a dinghy, or tender is towed or made fast.
point	To head close to the wind.
point of sail	The different angles from the wind on which a boat may sail; the boat's course relative to the direction of the wind.
port	The left-hand side of a boat, looking forward towards the bow (opposite of starboard).

port tack	When a boat sails with the main boom to starboard and wind hits the port side first.
privileged vessel	A boat that has the right-of-way (ROW).
R	
reach	Sailing on a tack with the wind roughly abeam, all sailing points between running and close- hauled.
ready about	Order to prepare for coming about.
reef	Reduce the sail area by folding or rolling surplus material on the boom or forestay.
rig	Arrangements of masts and sails.
rigging	Ropes and wire stays of a boat; securing masts and sails.
rudder	Vertical metal or wooden plate attached to the stern, whose movements steer the boat.
rules of the road	Right-of-way (ROW) regulations to prevent collisions between boats.
run	To sail with the wind aft and with the sheets eased out.
running rigging	All of the moving lines, such as sheets and halyards, used in the setting and trimming of sails.
S	
set	To hoist a sail.
shackle	A U-shaped piece of iron or steel with eyes in the ends, closed by a shackle pin.

sheave	A grooved wheel in a block or spar for a rope to run on.
sheet	Line that controls a sail or the movement of a boom.
ship shape	Neat, seamanlike.
shrouds	Transverse wires or ropes that support the mast laterally.
spar	Pole, mast, or boom that supports a sail.
spinnaker	A large, light, balloon-shaped sail set forward of the mainsail when running before the wind.
splice	To join ropes or wires by inlaying the strands and interweaving them.
spreaders	Horizontal spar attached to the mast, which extend the shrouds and stays and help to support the mast.
standing rigging	The shrouds and stays which are permanently set up and support the masts.
starboard	Right-hand side of a boat looking forward towards the bow (opposite of port).
starboard tack	Tack on which the wind strikes the starboard side first and the boom is out to port.
stay	Wire or rope which supports the mast in a fore-and-aft direction; part of the standing rigging.
staysail	Sail set on a stay inboard of the forward most sail.
step	A recess into which the fell of the mast is placed.
stern	After end of a boat.

stringer	A fore-and-aft member, fitted to strengthen the frames.
T	
tack	The lower forward corner of the sail, where the luff and the foot meet; also the diagonal made with the wind by a sailboat when close-hauled, (to change from one tack to another by coming about).
tacking	Working to windward by sailing close-hauled on alternate courses so that the wind is first on one side of the boat, then on the other.
tell-tales	Small lengths of wood sewn through a sail near the luff and leech to allow the air flow over the sail.
tender	See dinghy.
tiller	Short piece of wood by which the rudder is turned.
topsides	The part of a boat's hull which is above the waterline.
transom	A flat surface at the back of the hull to which the rudder is attached.
traveller	A slide which travels on a track and is used for altering sheet angles.
trim	To adjust the angle of the sails.
wake	A boat's track, behind.
waterline	The line along the hull at which a boat floats.
weather	Windward, opposite of leeward.

weather helm	Boat with a tendency to swing into the wind unless held on course.
weather side	The side of a boat on which the wind is blowing.
whisker pole	A light pole used to hold out the clew of a headsail when running.
winch	A mechanical device, consisting usually of a metal drum turned by a handle, around which a line is wound to give the crew more "help" when tightening a line.
windward	The direction from which the wind blows, towards the wind (opposite of leeward).

Created by Elizabeth Fox, an MLS student at
Rutgers University School of Communication, Information and Library Studies (SCILS)
Please send comments to elfox @scils.rutgers.edu
Last modified: December 16, 1997